PREY OF WAR

BY BRIAN GATTO

PREY OF WAR

WWW.SEVEREDPRESS.COM

ISBN: 978-1-923165-06-9

CHAPTER ONE

The war was over.

Spilling down the hill like water flowing from a stream, blood cascaded from human bodies into puddles of viscera. The fallen soldiers were eliminated in a most macabre way. They lay there, bleeding from bullet holes, riddled with them. The Vietnamese laughed, only shedding tears of joy.

Farmers turned stone cold killers, for them the war was not over. It would never be over so long as the Stalker Clan ruled this part of the deep jungle of North Vietnam. Their leader, Se-hun Wan, was as sadistic as a holocaust scientist and as cunning as a panther. He watched as his men gunned down the five POWs they had had locked up in the pits. They were growing tired and weak, useless to a man of his demands.

Three were dead. They would rot in the mud until eventually degrading into the earth. Their skin would mush at the touch and their meat would feed the insects and other wildlife. Two remained. Try as they might, they could not scale the hillside like their three fallen comrades had. None of his army were sure if it was because they physically couldn't or if they feared the outcome, they knew they'd inevitably face.

Se-hun puffed his chest and ordered them in English. "Turn around and come back!"

"Yeah! Come back!" Se-hun's younger brother, Ju-ho, chimed in. "We were just playing around."

"We'll buy ya a beer and have a grand old time!" one of his men shouted.

Since the arrival of the Americans, Philippine, and North Vietnamese, as well as a few others', culture had expanded, and many knew English now. At least sixty percent of Se-hun's small army could at least understand it. Thirty-eight out of one hundred and twelve men spoke it.

He kept meaning to hire tutors for his men, but the war always got in the way. Now that it was over it was only a matter of time.

"Turn and face us!" Se-hun shouted.

The two soldiers turned around slowly, not making eye contact. They would not give them dignity.

Daniel Stout turned to his brother, not only in arms but in blood, Ryan. "We can do this."

Ryan didn't say a word. He just nodded.

"Whoever makes it to the other side will live to see another day!" Se-hun explained.

His men turned to him in shock. It was almost an act of kindness to these intruders. Se-hun responded swiftly. "There are fates worse than death." He grinned.

They cheered and applauded in unison.

"Ready yourselves!" Se-hun raised his pistol to the sky and wasted no time firing.

The brothers ran for their lives. Bullets whizzed past their feet and caused small splashes all around them. Se-hun's men were clearly not aiming for them directly. They were only five yards away. Back to the 'safety' of the hard ground. Ju-ho raised his rifle and fired, hitting Ryan in the knee. He then went sprawling down, landing directly on a landmine.

An eruption of mud and blood coated Daniel in seconds. Pieces of his sibling were landing all around him. A string of intestine landed on his ear, wrapping around it.

Se-hun and his men cheered. Daniel landed on the ground and began to sob. He didn't care that he was naked and covered in filth. He was not afraid and only felt rage. He managed to calm himself and think rationally. There were twelve men around him, all carrying weapons. Blades as big as garter snakes, boots made for crushing skulls, guns used to kill and not wound.

Daniel got to his feet and stood before the commander who only smiled with his yellow-toothed grin. "That was quite the show."

The American didn't respond, nor did Se-hun need him to. "Alright, let's get back to the base!" he said and then repeated in several languages including Vietnamese, and Chinese.

Men from all over wanted to be a part of the Stalker Clan. Their reputation invoked only the harshest of killers to gather. The rules were simple. You were in or you die.

As long as the hike back was, none of the men complained. Not little brother Ju-ho, not fearless soldier Daniel, no one. They were rather silent the whole way back. A complete one-eighty from the landmine pit they were at earlier. The journey had been going on for a couple of hours now. Despite the raging heat and incessant bugs, Daniel stayed focused.

The four remaining members of his squad were back at the camp. He wondered if they were still alive. There was no telltale sign of how long they had been there. Originally, they were a twelve-man squad of death. One was killed in battle. They were eventually split up and captured. It felt like it had been a year, but, to Daniel, he was certain it had been at least a few months.

News of the war ending had reached them immediately. There was no celebration for them though. They were still behind enemy lines. Daniel hadn't seen his wife in two years. He hoped she'd wait for his return and not move on.

He now had no family to speak of out here in the sticks. His father, a hard ass drill sergeant, was taken out by an old dog who was from one of his earlier squads. He had leveled the whole camp, taking Cooper Stout and his new recruits in a massive ball of fire. Now Ryan was dead too. Daniel had very little drive left, but he still had Mary. She was waiting for him, she had to be. Otherwise, what was the point? The war was over; they had lost.

Suddenly, a Chinese soldier nudged him with the butt of his weapon. Daniel wanted to spin around, knock his face in. He stabilized himself and moved on. Instead of family in blood he had family in arms out there and four of them were back at the camp. At least, that's what he hoped.

It came from the sky and yet no one saw it through the dense foliage. Se-hun held up a fist and all his men crouched on their knees, the Chinese soldier pulling Daniel down in front of him. There were no familiar sounds, just a gust of wind that blew through the trees and caused the jungle to go silent.

Daniel knew better than to give away their position, even if it meant salvation.

After a short while, the breeze died down. The thick leafed trees stopped pressing forward and their fight with the unnatural occurrence came to an end. The brief cooling of the jungle was short lived as the sweltering heat began to invade the dense jungle again.

Se-hun lowered his hand and turned back to Daniel. A smile crept across the leader's face that was insidious and methodical. Like he was trying to come up with the best insult. Ju-ho spoke up first. "So close, yet so far. Huh, American?"

It was a weak insult, Se-hun thought, but it was enough to make Daniel visibly tense up and grind his teeth.

Se-hun suddenly felt something was off. It wasn't anything to do with the obvious overhead chopper or even his prisoner. His men were alert but seemed to be absent to the senses that he experienced. He had known this feeling before many times in his family's home camp. One of his cousins was killed by a prowling lion that had hunted the villagers. It must have been doing so for around a week given the signs of prints in the ground. In the days to come, three more children were taken until the beast was tracked and put down.

In the here and now, Se-hun felt the same way the night the second village kid was taken. He had been sleeping right next to him when the lion came in and snatched the poor boy without so much as a whimper to escape his mouth. Se-hun saw it though, and had reported it immediately.

Soon, he found himself looking for track indents on the ground. There were small ones from muskrats and other vermin, no big telltale signs. As he continued, Ju-ho noticed he was on edge. "What troubles you, brother?"

He wanted to tell him off, to shake the mortal fear that coiled around him like a python. There was no way of doing so at the current moment, a threat seemed all too apparent. "I think we're being watched."

"It's the jungle. It's alive with observant eyes."

Se-hun nodded. "I suppose you are right."

"We're almost back to the camp anyway. Shall I tell the men to break out the entertainment?"

The entertainment Ju-ho referred to was a radio from one of the prisoners. They were still back at the camp but without the joy of his tunes. Accompanying the man's belongings was a bag of cassette tapes. Every anti-Vietnam war, pro protest band that was big at the time was on them. Creedence Clearwater Revival, The Animals, and more. Se-hun didn't mind the music. It was like a big middle finger to Americans who were losing their minds over the pointless war. He nodded.

Ju-ho then looked to one of the men who carried the belongings and he grinned from ear to ear. He pulled the radio out from a bag and inserted one of the tapes into the deck. Where the cassette left off was at the last seconds of the song *War Pigs* by Black Sabbath. The next song, *Paranoid,* kicked on. The high then low swings of the guitar intro brought the spirit back to the group. Then the reverb on the guitars and Ozzy's booming voice made them want to stop what they were doing and start dancing.

They knew their place and where they were and were able to compose themselves. They'd save it for the big show back at the camp that night.

Their leader felt the song was symbolic of how he was feeling. He must have been as paranoid as the song title suggested to him. His brother was also right. The jungle was full of tricks for the mind. Everything was hunky dory now. He looked over his shoulder at Daniel and almost froze in place. The look of absolute hatred covered his face. If looks could kill, Se-hun would be afraid. The man's expression was downright sinister.

After a couple of minutes, *Planet Caravan* came on and the soft melancholy of the beat was mesmerizing. Se-hun didn't like it because it seemed to dampen his senses. However, his small army of men seemed to be soothed by its tone. To him the song was eerie, to them it was cathartic.

They came upon the first obstacle. It was a river the locals referred to as raging rapids. For Se-hun and his men, it was a once-a-week trek. For most though, it'd be the ultimate test of stability and leg power. Daniel didn't show much emotion when they were heading to the landmine pit, and he showed even less now. No one looked back or gave it a second thought. Everyone charged into the river and trudged across. Holding their weapons above their heads made it hard to keep balance but if Se-hun could do it then so could they.

After twenty minutes the group was across. They walked a mere five yards only to come up to the second river, the Flowing Falls. The river led to a huge waterfall that had at least a sixty-foot drop. Few farmers dared to travel this way. Not only because of the Stalker Clan being in the territory but because the very strong current claimed far too many lives. It would sweep them right from under their feet and carry them to their tumbling deaths.

This time was different. It wasn't that one of the men couldn't take the surging water. Instead, something bit him. Se-hun, Ju-ho, Daniel and the other men spun around to see the Chinese soldier flailing about in frothing red water. He was the other guy who egged Daniel and his brother to run back to the group. As far as Daniel was concerned, this was justified.

"Piranha?!" Ju-ho shouted.

Before Se-hun could answer, the soldier split in two as if he were cut through like butter. There was a swift action that made the upper half of his body fall into the river to be swept away. His bottom half was nowhere to be seen.

The soldier standing next to Ju-ho was ordered to check it out and he quickly went to investigate. He expected to feel tiny teeth tearing into his soft flesh. Maybe an overwhelming sensation of being swarmed and devoured. Instead, there was nothing. The water was lukewarm from all the blood and the soldier placed his hand in it. When he pulled it back, it was black and red, stained with his comrade's blood. Quickly, he ran back to his squad, slinking back in utter disgust.

"He's gone," the soldier said.

"It had to be piranha!" Ju-ho cried out. "Let's get out of the river, now!"

"I don't think it was," Daniel chimed in. "That didn't look like any fish attack I've ever seen."

To Se-hun's surprise, some of his own men nodded and muttered in agreement. He took his colt commander and shot the other soldier who went in to investigate the attack in the shoulder. As his man fell backwards into the water, blood began to form around him. It was coming directly from his wound. "You see! If there were piranha, he'd be a dead man already!"

"Then what's in the water?" Daniel asked.

Again, Se-hun's men seemed to gravitate towards the prisoner's observation. Se-hun was enraged with jealousy and pointed the gun at Daniel. "Shut up, you! He must've just stepped on a trap."

Daniel didn't argue further. He knew his place whether he liked it or not.

Wordlessly, they carried on. Soon they were out of the river and heading for a hillside. This was Se-hun's least favorite part. Mainly because of the strenuous work he'd have to do to complete the obstacle. He swore to himself he would take a horse next time. Suddenly, two trucks drove past them to the right. Four of his men were in them. One got out to offer Se-hun a seat.

"No, I am walking with the men today," Se-hun said proudly.

His men nodded and drove back to make their way around the mountain. It was quicker by vehicle but would take much longer to cover the distance by foot. The hill was the best option.

As Se-hun started his ascent, his men followed without hesitation or grief. Daniel wanted to get in that truck but knew he'd be shot down if he even suggested the thought. The climb took half an hour. Soon they reached the peak and Se-hun looked over the area with a sense of accomplishment. The camp, the river below, the surrounding jungle. It was all his, he commanded it, he owned it.

An empire.

Daniel stared at it with grim reservation. It was a rather small camp with a massive, thatched roof covering a portion of it for recreational activities. There were eight huts, and one house-sized shelter that was Se-hun's palace. It was a disgusting pit of hay and mud.

"Welcome home!" Se-hun shouted out to everyone, including Daniel, much to his disdain.

CHAPTER TWO

They were noticed immediately.

Opening the gates to the prison camp, Anton, Se-hun's Russian right-hand man, grinned with excitement. The feeling of a horrible gut-punch entered Daniel as he saw the look of the cold-blooded killer's face. It could only mean one of two things. One of the prisoners was dead or dying. The other being he was about to get whatever he wanted. If one of his comrades were hurt, he wondered if Anton was responsible. There was no way to tell now. He'd probably be executed for asking.

Se-hun approached his assassin who leaned over and whispered into his right ear. The other ear was open to hear any comments from his men about what was going on. He heard what he wanted on both sides: sex, and silence.

Anton then looked past Se-hun and at Daniel. The prisoner was disheveled and covered in mud but still had a face of rage. There was no intimidation behind his eyes. Anton wanted to take that away from him, to strip him of prowess and humiliate him in front of his remaining men.

"Looks like our good fortune will continue tonight!" Se-hun cheered. "Two beautiful women will be here within the next couple of hours for our pleasure!"

There was rousing applause along with whooping and hollering.

"*Jamaes*!" Se-hun shouted.

Daniel was disgusted by the piggish behavior when the men were told that the women were sisters. He didn't speak much of the foreign languages common in this area, but he knew that word given that he helped rescue a pair of sisters from a raid on a village five years ago. The father was forever grateful and told him *geudeul-eun jamaeyeyo* - they're sisters. He went on to say they should never be apart.

As he remained in thought, Anton approached. He grabbed Daniel by the neck which alarmed him. His quick decision-making helped him to not fight back despite the sudden shock that shot through his body. Then he was guided towards his home away from home.

From inside the fenced-off hole in the dirt, a cage that could barely fit two men let alone five, Ace Whitaker was the first to notice Dainel's solo return. He was happy to see his commanding officer had made it. The grim expression on his face showed that he had been the only one, which infuriated Ace as well as Rex Forbes. Both were once built like concrete and tough as nails. As time went on their muscular build turned into nothing more than flabby excess skin.

Vinnie Garcia woke from a nightmare when the cage door opened. He screamed like a madman and instinctively reached down for his sidearm which had been taken away when they were first captured. Daniel was thrust into the cage on the floor in front of him.

The only one who had remained calm during their stay in the death camp was Saber, a Filipino carried over from the Vietnam campaign. He had been the smallest yet swiftest of the group. There were two teeth on each side of his mouth that were longer than the others, hence the nickname. No one knew his real title.

Saber held out his hand and helped Daniel up. He could only be hunched over, for his whole six-foot-two height was too tall for the cage, which was about four feet high and ten feet deep. "Thank you," Daniel told Saber.

His comrade nodded and then went back to a relaxed state, meditating.

"How can you be so calm?" Vinnie shouted at Saber who didn't acknowledge him.

'You need to control yourself, soldier," Daniel shot at his navigator.

Besides being able to read a map properly, Vinnie was dead weight. His short fuse and incessant complaining were part of the reason they were in the mess they were in now. The other being a case of being at the wrong place at the wrong time.

None of them knew this camp existed.

Ace began over towards Daniel. "I'm sorry about the rest of the team, including your brother."

Daniel nodded, holding back a few tears. "They were all troopers. Those sick bastards out there knew all along that only one would make it and that one was me."

Rex overheard and pounded his fist on the cage. "We went from a fully functioning unit down to five men in less than three months! Hell, our numbers were just cut in half this morning. What're they planning? Why are they doing this?!"

"They're playing games, man," Vinnie said with a jittery shake. "I hate games!"

Daniel thought for a moment. "I have an idea. It's thin, paper-thin, but it just might work."

Everyone, including Saber, looked up to their leader.

"I overheard that two tramps, sisters, are coming into the camp today."

"A little money for the honeys? So what?" Rex growled.

"Maybe we can convince them to let us out of here," Daniel suggested.

"Right? No offense, sir, I think you've been out in the sun too long." Vinnie chuckled and coughed for the effort.

"I have a feeling this'll work. Call it a hunch," Daniel said.

He was not about to tell his remaining men that he hoped that the two sisters were the ones he had rescued during a raid. It was the last line of hope he had, a small chance that could lead to salvation. *Maybe I am going mad.*

"We're going to let you off here!" the pilot shouted into his mic-piece.

His co-pilot got off his chair and made his way over towards the man sitting on a bench before him. In the cockpit, Eddie Stokes was looking over his gear. As he checked his water supply again, the co-pilot secured the cable to a notch on the helicopter floor.

Eddie then got up and attached the hook around his belt. The pilot spoke into the mic again. "We'll be back to pick you up in two days. Meet us here at the rendezvous point."

Their passenger gave him the thumbs up and then hopped off the aircraft. He propelled down with grace. The line kept shelling out, going and going. At the last possible moment, it snapped in place and made a cracking sound as it pressed against the notch.

Unclipping himself, Eddie landed on his hands and knees in a patch of thick plants and then looked back to the helicopter. The wave goodbye was the sendoff that always made him feel most alone. Here he was, in the Vietnam jungle, armed with nothing more than a service revolver given to him by his dad and a camera.

There was stupid is and then there was stupid does. Right now, he felt like he was working towards both of those attributes.

The heat of the jungle caused him to start sweating instantaneously. There was no comfort to be found in the swaying trees or the occasional drop of rainwater. Everything natural made him feel hotter. His fifty extra pounds of weight didn't agree with the jungle. He was at least sixty pounds above his body mass index.

Over time, the trek became more tolerable as the view opened in front of him. It wasn't a pleasant hike, but it was doable. He knew if he kept to the tree line then he'd more than likely be out of view of the Vietcong.

As the day wore on, he began to feel lonesome. It was probably the long nights of going through polaroids and rolls of film that made him feel alone most of the time. Still, he had a job to do. *Expose the exposed* his editor would say. It basically meant leave no stone unturned at all costs.

Eventually, he ran out of the field and began to work his way back into the jungle. He stopped dead in his tracks as he heard two vehicles approaching fast. Crouching on his knees as they ached with each bend, he found himself sweating profusely. It was worse than before.

By the sounds of it, two mopeds were driving in his direction. Eddie didn't want to risk taking a picture, so he quickly pulled out his Leica flex video camera and assembled it as fast as humanly possible. He had just fed the filmstrip through when he saw the bikes. There were two Asian women, one on each. They were driving cautiously but seemed to be enjoying the jungle air.

One had shoulder-length black hair while the other's hair went all the way down her back. They looked like siblings, but Eddie couldn't be sure. He always had a hard time telling them apart. It wasn't that he didn't want to either. Still, the one with the long flowing hair was beyond beautiful. Her lightly tanned skin had a glitter on it that accentuated her strong cheek bones and thin nose.

Both women were dressed in one-piece, satin jumpsuits of sorts. They were almost midriffs, but a patch of material ran down their backs. Their mid-sections in front were completely exposed. One of the suits was pink which belonged to the long-haired woman while the other was yellow. Each had some floral prints on them.

Eddie watched as the two drove by and then disappeared from view. He realized then that he hadn't recorded anything. For a reason he couldn't fathom, he was just honored to see them in his memory. He then packed up his camera.

Saber felt something was off. It wasn't that he was stuck as a prisoner in a death camp, nor was it Vinnie's consistent nightmares keeping everyone awake and alert, preventing them from their own sleep. There was something else. Nagging away at him like a child wanting a toy they can't have, it annoyed Saber. It was not so much that the disturbance was a pest, rather it was that he couldn't figure out why it was bothering him.

Deep in meditation, he began to do more deep breathing. There were a few groans during his exhales and Vinnie looked on with an agitated glare. Just then, Saber's eyes shot open. They were wide and white. Vinnie could see the red veins bulging out on the bottom. His pupils then became visible again but were soon glazed over with a white film of sorts. They were hazy but clearly darting back and forth.

"Yo, what the hell's gotten into Saber?!" Vinnie shouted.

Ace, Rex, and Daniel ran to the wild-eyed man just as he began to spasm.

"Let's lay him on his back," Ace suggested.

"No!" Daniel protested. "If he's convulsing, he might swallow his tongue if he is on the ground."

Their commander then did something unpredictable. He slapped Saber across the face, smacking the devilish act right out of him.

It took a few minutes before Saber fully recovered. In that time, Vinnie was biting his fingernails, what was left of them. He had been writing tallies in the dirt of how many of them had perished. The dedication cost him a few fingernails.

A howl of horror came as Saber shot forward. He was weak and disoriented but alive.

"What going on in there?" the guard approached, asking in broken English.

"Bad dream," Vinnie told him. "Now he knows my pain."

CHAPTER THREE

They were early.

Jemma Reyes and her sister, Agwa, had one goal for tonight. They had to ensure satisfaction. As their mother would say, *they had to make their customers happy and collect.* Their father had been the same way. It was a rigorous job that required many sleepless nights and states of exhaustion. Somebody had to put food on the table, and they were two, tired bodies.

As they pulled up to the gate, the guard had a noticeable shoulder wound. He didn't bring any attention to it, nor would they pay him any mind. The Stalker Clan were known for their stoic, emotionless perseverance. Still, Agwa couldn't help but wonder why he had a bullet wound. They knew Se-hun had no time for weak men. Unless he caused the injury himself.

The two Vietcong standing at the gate did search the women. Both copped a feel under their breasts and squeezed in between their thighs. They didn't test their luck further and the sisters were allowed to pass. They drove their mopeds into the camp without a second thought. Once they entered, the whistling began.

Agwa suddenly felt ill. She didn't want to have to do this again. She had only been to two camps prior. The first was worse than the second with a savage gang rape of her innocence. Things could always get worse though. It was something she didn't want to experience again.

Jemma looked over her shoulder and smiled. "Last one, that was the deal."

Agwa took a deep breath and nodded.

The men approached and began to touch their hands. Every one of them was aroused but some were harder to tell than others. Jemma thought it was pathetic.

"Attention!" Ju-ho shouted over the crowd.

Silence.

Se-hun walked outside of his 'palace' and down the moldy stone steps. "How nice of you to come, ladies!"

"You know the rules, pay up front," Jemma said.

Grimy, yellow teeth appeared through his thin-lipped grin as Se-hun pulled out a wad of cash. He threw it at Jemma who took it without hesitation, catching it in midair.

"Park your little toy bikes around the corner as we prepare the entertainment for the night to come!" Se-hun explained.

Jemma and Agwa did as they were instructed to. They were not able to mask the look of dread on their faces though, which turned some of the soldiers on. Agwa scoffed in disgust.

"Don't worry, ladies!" one of the Chinese soldiers smiled. "I'll put some nice music on to set the mood!"

Day became night as a skinned boar was cooked over the fireplace. The apple in its mouth was starting to crisp as Anton carved out a piece of its hide. He stuffed it into his mouth. The uncooked pig's juice spilled down his chin. Salivating over the next bite, he reached for another chunk. Ju-ho was quick to intervene and smack his hand away. "Patience, you animal." "We're all animals! Some are just more fragile than others!" He stroked up the kid's hair and then rubbed his hands in it.

Again, Ju-ho shooed him off.

"As for me," Anton began to parade around, "I'm a carnivore. I eat my meat how I want it! If I want it bloody raw then so be it!"

"Not tonight," Ju-ho chuckled. "You'll just have to be patient."

Anton didn't like to be told what to do but what was he to do? Ju-ho was the kid brother of his boss. If Se-hun weren't around though, he'd make sure Ju-ho would pay for his arrogance. Anton then stormed off towards the cage.

Daniel looked up to see the hulking Vietnamese goon talking to the guard outside. He was motioning for him to head down to the party. Without hesitation, he quickly made his way down the small hill. Anton then turned to the cage.

"I'll give you one more week. By then, you'll all probably be either dead or killed."

"How much you wanna bet?" Daniel spat.

Just then, Anton reached down and unsheathed a scimitar out of its holder. He pointed the curved blade at Daniel's throat. "I bet that you won't make it the next two days. If you do, we'll square off and, whoever wins will get this here fine blade."

"Done deal." Daniel smiled.

"If I make it, I want my goddamn radio back," Rex snarled.

"This isn't a negotiation. This is a game between me and your commanding officer. Or shall I say, demoted officer," Anton chuckled.

"Come on, man. Get that squinty-eyed China man up here and let him and I have a talk!" Rex laughed.

"Ha! In your present condition, I doubt you'll even be able to stand to meet him eye to eye. I hope your night is swell." Anton said and then unzipped his pants. He began to urinate inside the cage. Daniel wanted to rip his puny privates off but thought better of it.

Thankfully, the assassin didn't stick around for much longer. He soon left the prisoners in peace. Peace was hard to come by and even when it did it was short lived. The sounds of crickets, frogs, and jungle creatures brought about a sense of comfort.

For Rex, it was a feeling of longing. He missed being back home in Louisiana. His property, gun collection, and, most of all, wife were all but a fog at the moment. When he was drafted, he promised her he'd come home in one piece. She had told him that she just wanted him back alive.

During the assignment phase, the enlisted personnel was given the title: communications officer. He was a ground specialist in that field. He ran with the troops and carried a weapon, but he wasn't a solider. He was hard as stone though and proficient at combat much like the rest of the squad but his background in, of all things, his hometown radio show seemed to fit the bill for the position. They needed someone who was able to not only reach out to headquarters but knew how to operate the machinery.

He had found friendship in Ace as well as another fellow by the name of Barney Cook. He had perished early on and was the first casualty of the group. He wasn't brought to the camp but was more of a warning kill. It told them that if anyone stepped out-of-line, they'd be slaughtered.

All Rex had in the world out here was his music and the enemy had taken that away from him. Killed that from him along with Barney. He wasn't sure how much longer he could take it.

Then, as if to add insult to injury, he heard a tune start to play. It jolted him out of memory lane. The slow build up of the drums followed by the sexy guitar riff echoed from afar somewhere in the camp as *Susie Q* by Creedence Clearwater Revival began to play. John Fogerty's powerful voice cast a tear that was jerked from Rex's eye.

The enemy had set up speakers and placed the radio right next to the receiver. Their laughter could be heard by Se-hun who was ready to start the festivities. He gave the order to Anton who began to light some tiki torches around the camp.

The orange flame cast a warm hue across the greenery.

Mood set, Se-hun looked around the camp. He spotted the sisters trying to avoid conversing with his men. He stared directly at Jemma who took the hint and began to approach. Agwa quickly grabbed her hand and whined something that Se-hun couldn't hear.

Jemma muttered something. He was decent at reading lips and could of sworn she said *last time*. She then managed to pry her hand free and then strolled up to the 'palace'.

Daniel only caught a glimpse of the top of Jemma's head. Her jet-black hair was parted almost all the way down the middle. He couldn't be sure if she was who he was looking for, but he prayed she was.

When Se-hun took her by the hand and guided her inside, he played up the charm angle. Jemma knew it wouldn't last long and that she'd be assaulted. She owed it to herself and to her family to stay composed and willing.

Ju-ho and Anton both looked at each other. Their hate towards one another subsided as they cheered. They, along with three other men, began to surround Agwa. Playing with her hair and copping feels, they would say things like *tight lady* and *no sister to save you now*.

Agwa began to scream as they clawed at her. She cried out for her sister as Se-hun shut the door to the palace.

"Tell me, how old is your sister?" Se-hun inquired.

"It's not important."

"I asked you a very simple question and I expect an answer, bitch!" His charm was already wearing off.

Jemma frowned. "Fifteen."

"She's awfully young to be putting herself out there."

"If there was another way to make good money she wouldn't."

"Well, if you perform well, both of you, I may give a little bonus out of the kindness of my heart," Se-hun said, placing a hand over his chest.

Jemma sighed just as *I Put a Spell on You* came on. It startled her because of the instant banging of the drums. Se-hun placed a hand on her shoulder and rubbed it. The satin crop-top aroused him but he contained his excitement.

"Dance for me." He grinned.

She looked at him, her eyes like daggers. She then backed away and began to sway her hips. Her stomach then began to roll slightly as she did a belly dance. Her hip-hugging bell bottoms moved perfectly with her frame and her hair motioned back and forth. Her eyes never left him out of pure hatred, but he didn't care.

Se-hun approached but Jemma put up one finger signaling him to wait, be patient. She then turned around and leaned over, shaking her rear in front of him. He saw how nice and round her cheeks were and just wanted to bury his face in them.

He looked down at her white platforms and saw her small feet moving back and forth in a cutesy fashion. She maneuvered in a way that showed she had full control of her muscles. He had never seen a woman like her before. She was distractingly beautiful.

To her full effect.

She quickly spun around and jammed a blade into Se-hun's shoulder. The man stumbled back and fell, hitting his head on a wooden chair near the middle of the room. Blood began to pour from his cranium as Jemma lay on top of him.

"Was it as good for you as it was for me?" She grinned insidiously.

There was a sudden change, a shift in the night air. The squishy sound of a mushy object squelched and popped from under her. It wasn't coming from Se-hun but rather below the hut. She lay motionless as the floorboards creaked. It then ceased and everything returned to normal.

And then she heard the first sound of discomfort.

"The bastards are listening to my greatest hits tape," Rex sighed. "I had it imported from home when CCR had it released."

"It's just music," Vinnie insisted.

"That's like saying sex is just feeling," Rex snapped back.

"Whatever," Vinnie said as he rested his head on the dirt floor ready for another nightmare-filled dreamscape.

"I wonder where the sentry is," Daniel thought.

Saber opened one eye to look out past the bamboo bars. To most, it was nothing, just a late return for the guard. It would be understandable given the festivities. For Saber it was a crucial moment of clarity. "Something's happened."

"One could only hope," Ace chuckled.

There was silence for a few more minutes. The post had been abandoned for a while now. Vinnie began to get ideas. "Maybe this is our chance."

A man then began to stumble up the hill. He was walking funny, rather tipsy. He tripped over his own feet and clutched his throat. Finally collapsing, the sentry fell on a post and lay against his back. He was gurgling.

"Damn fool can't handle his liquor," Rex laughed.

"Like I said, this could be our chance!" Vinnie said, annoyed.

"What do you propose?" Daniel inquired.

"We dig," Saber said sternly.

He untucked his crossed legs and crawled over towards the gate. He then plunged his fingers into the mushy dirt and began pulling handfuls of mud out.

Vinnie wasted no time running hunched over to help, never minding his ripped and bruised fingers. There was only room for two people to be situated in that spot and they dug feverishly. One for freedom, one for safety.

Saber felt something had happened and that it was no longer safe anywhere in the camp. Vinnie didn't see that and just wanted to be free of their imprisonment. Either way, both men's fingertips were bleeding and scrapes covered their hands. They had the same end goal: escape.

Suddenly, an explosion shook the ground and the music soon cut out.

Eddie Slater had made it far in life being an honest journalist. That wasn't something many in his field could say. His time in the streets of New York City, trying to uncover hidden corruption, was short lived. He pushed too far and was told, rather forcefully, to leave.

It wasn't until Eddie went to the cinema and saw a vigilante movie, *Death Wish*, last year that he felt his true calling in life. He wanted to be a journalist with an edge. He carried a piece where he went and knew how to use it. If things got out of hand, he'd record the act of defending himself and then take witness statements after to enforce the legitimacy of his innocence.

If a little provoking had to be incurred, then so be it. He would never go after someone unless he was completely convinced of their crimes. He had been sticking with the act for a year now. The shtick never got old. He uncovered more than he ever thought capable.

One time, he found out that there was an experiment being conducted on fish that involved gene splicing, but he never got close enough to uncover it all. They moved operations to Mexico for a few months before cutting their losses. Or so the media and public believed. He was certain the tests were still going on right here in North Vietnam.

Camp was set and he was resting a hotdog over a fire, the smaller the better. He didn't want to risk being caught by enemy forces that still roamed the area. The war was over, but the territory was still a terrible terrain for traveling and enemy forces.

With the weenie roast complete, he let it cool off for a few seconds before taking a bite. In those few seconds, his whole angle changed. He would put aside the literal fishy story and begin to investigate a massive explosion that occurred about ten kilometers from his camp.

"What in the shit!" he screamed.

He dropped his hotdog on a stick into the fire and quickly grabbed his Nikon.

"Oh, thank god!" He looked it over and was grateful that it was already set to go from the false alarm with the women.

Aiming the camera upward, he stood up and recorded the fireball that illuminated the jungle in an orange glow.

CHAPTER FOUR

No one knew.

The massive explosion erupted from an unknown source. One minute the men were having a wonderful time, defiling the young woman, drinking, eating, the next everything went wrong. A fireball shot upward as the wind rushed through the camp. It was strong enough to sweep several dozen people off their feet.

After the initial chaos ensued, the men tried to recollect themselves. They got to their feet and quickly made their way to the munitions bunker. A couple of the sentries in the towers in front of the camp were scanning the area for hostile targets.

In one of the other huts the despicable act was taking place. After the explosion, Anton and Ju-ho ran outside, the former dragging Agwa out by her neck. The three other men were still pulling up their pants when a second explosion occurred. This time, it was a direct hit on the hut, but it wasn't one of fire.

A massive, plant-like organism shot upward and engulfed the hut in a massive maw. Ju-ho spun around and stifled a scream as vines were uprooted and reached inside the hut. They took hold of the three men and sliced them to bits. The extensions were like blades cutting through butter.

One of the guerrillas ran towards the speaker system to sound the alarm. He grabbed the nearby radio and tossed it onto the ground, smashing it. With the receiver in hand, he was about to alert his comrades when a root expelled from the ground and stabbed him in the throat. Tiny vines punctured through his neck as he felt an unfathomable pain rising from within him. Soon, leaves began to grow and were coming out of his mouth.

"*Dang xảy ra*?!" one of the Vietnamese soldiers shouted.

Anton nodded in agreement. *Just what in the hell* is *going on?*

Screams could be heard coming from the munitions bunker as blood sprayed out the entrance. It showered the stones and plants around it. The fauna seemed to be absorbing the crimson liquid.

"Brother!" Ju-ho shouted.

Se-hun did not respond. He was nowhere to be seen.

Anton, despite hating Ju-ho for being a little punk, honored Se-hun's wishes to protect him. He grabbed the kid and carried both him and Agwa towards the watchtowers. As they ran, more roots came up and impaled guerrillas in all different places. One was pierced through the back and out his chest, another was impaled through the groin and upward out his mouth.

Agwa was in shock. She did not utter Jemma's name. She couldn't fathom what was happening now let alone what could have happened to her sister. She ran with the two men but didn't see them as evil as they were. They were like cowardly children running in fright. She looked around and noticed that all the men were running like frightened chickens. Some were waving their arms. In reality they were alerting whomever they could of the impending danger, to Agwa they were flapping their wings.

She began to giggle. Anton noticed this and wanted to ditch her but remembered she was the perfect shield. Lightweight enough to be maneuvered easily, she was the perfect defense.

They reached the watchtower on the right, the sentries waving for them to come up. Ju-ho wasted no time in going first. Anton allowed Agwa to go ahead of him, but he would be right behind her. He was thankful that she ascended quickly.

When they reached the top, one of the sentries began firing behind them. The roots with their sinister vines were climbing up after them. Yellowish liquid squirted out as bullets riddled the twigs and bark. The other sentry decided to join his comrade in attempting to eradicate the ever-growing plants but sensed something was off. The feeling of being watched came over him like a sharp breeze chilling one to their bones. He spun around but there was nothing there. He gave his eyes a few more seconds to adjust and then decided to look through the trees.

There was something there. A hideous figure. Its arms were raised as if it were cheering. It was not doing such a gesture. In the line of view from the arms, coming up from the ground, were the roots.

Whatever that thing was, it was controlling the plants.

Quick to react, the sentry aimed his issued AK47 and fired at the bipedal abomination. A series of holes appeared in its chest, and it fell backwards.

All stopped then.

The roots seemed to shrivel up and die, the vines quickly rotted in place and lay limp on the ground. Some of them receded while others remained.

A sense that it was all over overcame the sentry responsible for the fatal finish of the forest figure. He cheered and then ran over towards the hatch.

"What are you doing?!" Anton grabbed him by the shoulder.

"I killed it! Now I go claim my prize!" The Vietnamese soldier smirked.

Anton looked to the other sentry who shrugged and followed his companion down the ladder.

Both soldiers looked to the other duo in the second watchtower and gave them the thumbs up. They returned the gesture. Soon, all four sentries, the protectors of the camp, left it all together and ventured out into the jungle, locking the gate behind them. It didn't take long to find the yellow liquid, the broken trees, and the footprints. The body was mysteriously absent.

Daniel had been worried before but now he was downright nervous. Saber and Vinnie were still digging, and the guard remained unconscious. Ace was afraid, the explosion followed by gunfire made him curious, but, when it all stopped, that's what terrified him. He wasn't sure if they won or if the invading forces were successful. Even if they were there to wipe out the camp, who was to say they'd save them.

"They better not have broken my radio," Rex snarled.

"Is that all you care about right now?!" Ace looked over his shoulder.

"It's all I have."

"You still have your life," Ace added. "That is just a piece of junk you can get at a pawnshop. Make it back home to your wife and then spend some money on a new one."

There was momentary silence.

"So you think it's broken?" Rex asked.

Ace just glared at his brother in arms.

Just then, the guard moved. Saber and Vinnie stopped digging at the sudden motion. It was an odd movement, like he hiccuped but the sound never came out. He then began gagging and convulsing. It went on for a full minute before he stopped.

Then came the ripping sound. Flesh separating and clothes tearing, something was coming out of him. Vinnie began to holler in fear. It looked like tentacles were popping out of his chest. Daniel realized quickly that they were more floral than that, almost like roots from a tree.

Pop pop pop.

A few shots could be heard and then entered the guardsman's body. The petrified prisoners shook with fear. This was it; they were too late. Another enemy would come, and they'd take them all out. Rex and Daniel prayed for forgiveness to their wives while Ace thought about his kid brother in Arkansas and how he'd be alone with his sick mother after news came back about his own death. Their aunt wouldn't stick around after that. He promised he'd be home to help after the war to relieve her of duty. Vinnie was jittery but in his maddened state he did recollect a pretty young woman he wanted to ask out at the market down the street from where he lived. He had a purpose to make it back and start a future. Saber had a family back home, but his prime objective now was to survive.

Then, a shadow appeared, cast by the fire within the camp, and began to grow larger and larger as the figure approached. It then shrank down as the individual came into view.

They came to the makeshift prison and saw the men, cowering, covering their eyes in prayer or fear.

"Commander Stout?" a female's voice could be heard.

Daniel responded to his title and looked to see it was a woman. She had long, straight, parted black hair with a slutty outfit on. "Oh, thank God!"

"Who's this?" Ace inquired.

"I'm hoping that it's my plan coming to fruition."

The woman quickly leaned to the guardsman, inspecting him. There was no doubt he was dead, but those things inside could still be alive. She had to be careful. With her manicured hands and two-inch fingernails, she dug into his pockets. As she did, the material on his tan uniform shifted. Blood was spilling on his khakis and covering the ground around him. Finally, she produced the keys. She then ran over and put one of them into the lock. After some jiggling, she deduced it was the wrong one. There were three more keys to try.

A wave of explosions echoed through the camp as gunshots rang out. Daniel realized they were AK47s and that they were more than likely being used by the Vietcong soldiers.

"Get us out of here!" Vinnie cried.

"What's going on out there, lady?!" Rex asked.

"I honestly don't know, and my name is Jemma!" she explained.

She tried the second and then the third key. They didn't work either. More shots erupted, sounds of chaos in the night. Screaming could soon be heard. Jemma tried the last key, but it still didn't work. "These aren't the right keys!"

"Try them again!" Vinnie cried out.

The screams stopped and Jemma looked over her shoulder. She then looked back at the soldiers. "There's no time! Back as far away from the door as you can!"

Obeying the woman who was now running back to the guard, the men sat silent. Jemma picked up the dead man's AK47 and ran back. She stopped halfway to put some distance between herself and the cage door. There was no reason to get herself injured nor any of the men. She aimed and quickly fired, blowing the lock off the door.

It snapped off with a clinking sound and fell to the dirt below. A sense of relief fell over the five men as they began to climb for the exit of their home away from home for the last few months.

Jemma ran to them and opened the cage. She pulled out Vinnie who insisted on going first. No one argued, the man was clearly losing his mind or had already lost it. When he got out, he tried to stand upright but collapsed onto the ground. He hadn't been out of the cage in a month.

Daniel came second, having just been out in the morning. He assisted Jemma in helping Rex and Ace out. Saber was last, he had never left the prison. He had to crawl on his hands and knees even when outside of the cage.

Daniel went to help him up. "Come on, brother. Let's go home!"

His back and shoulders made some popping sounds, but Saber fought through the uncomfortable pain. The five remaining members of the original squad helped each other the best they could. Jemma took point and was proficient in keeping them out of the way of potential enemies.

They rounded the corner and marched through the patch that passed as a garden, stepping on tomatoes and berry bushes. Then, they heard a shout.

Jemma looked over her shoulder and told them to crouch low by waving her hand down. She then scouted out the area and saw Ju-ho running in their direction. Anton was about thirty feet behind. He was at the watchtower helping Agwa down off the ladder.

Before Ju-ho could round the corner to the cage, he took a sharp right and ended up directly in front of Jemma. She quickly hopped up and pointed the AK47 at his face. Anton had already started running over and didn't have time to rummage through his comrade's belongings for a weapon.

"Stop where you are!" Jemma shouted.

Anton did so but Agwa kept running towards her sister. Soon, she was past Ju-ho and behind her with the other men.

"What're ya doin', lady?"

"I'm here to rain on your parade!"

Both Anton and Ju-ho looked around. It appeared as though all their men were dead, killed by some foreign enemy to not only the territory but the planet.

Just then, a figure leapt over the wall and soared through the air. It was seemingly projected forward by a catapult. In reality, it was propelled by simply pushing itself off the ground. Jemma watched as the ariel enemy stopped in midair and shot out roots into all different directions. Then it punctured through thatched roofs and stuck into the ground. Soon, it was hovering over them and lowering itself down towards Jemma.

She wasted no time and pointed the weapon at the creature. As it got closer, she made sure to aim for the center of the forehead. She fired with an impressive report that made the recoil hurt Jemma's shoulder. After a dozen shots the creature fell to the earth.

Without missing a beat, she trained the weapon back onto Ju-ho and Anton. "I've got plenty more where that came from!" Surprisingly, the two men hadn't budged when they had the opportunity. The beast was descending upon the trap, and they just stood in place. Anton cursed himself for that.

"Move!" she told them.

Vinnie kept close to Agwa and Jemma. He wasn't going far from any ally that had a gun.

Ace and Daniel looked for weapons over by the munitions bunker. Ace found an M1 carbine with an M4 bayonet at the end while Daniel found an M2 flamethrower complete with a backpack and fuel tank. Both were found right outside on men who almost had a chance to fight.

They struggled to get them on. Their bodies, mostly their lower backs and shoulders, ached with searing pain.

Rex limped over to the speaker system, his legs felt like pins and needles, and saw his radio. It was busted. The tape deck was loose and one of the covers for the speaker had popped off. He sat on his knees and wanted to cry. He thought back to what Ace had told him. *My wife needs me more than this radio.* He got up and joined Vinnie.

Saber looked over the body of the creature. It looked like a tree but with a humanoid shape.

Furthermore, it had qualities that wouldn't be out of the realm of a monster. It had triangular, wooden teeth and black pupils. Its head was particularly combed shape that led to a slight point at the top. He turned it over and saw something that made his blood run cold. There was a dorsal fin on the back.

"What is this thing, Saber?!" Daniel's voice made Saber jump in place.

He looked at his commanding officer with dark, terrified eyes. "It's unnatural. I've never seen anything like it before."

"Is it a plant, an alien?" Ace wondered as he walked up behind Daniel.

"It's an invader," Saber said coldly. "Maybe alien, maybe from Earth but not meant to be. It just doesn't make sense."

"Well, it's dead now and we need to get a move on."

Saber nodded and got up. The three men made their way back towards the group who were stopped at the gate for some reason.

"What's going on?" Daniel shouted after them."We need keys," Jemma explained.

"Don't they have any?"

"Even if they did, I doubt they'd give us them," Jemma stated.

Daniel thought back. "Hold on, what about those keys on the guardsman?"

Jemma sighed. "I didn't bring them with me." "I'll get them," Rex said and then weakly jogged towards the cages, trying to fight through the pain.

"Ace go with him," Daniel instructed.

The soldier did not argue as he turned and sluggishly joined after Rex. The two ran side by side as if it were a training exercise, only if they were at the end of it, drained and tired. They rounded the corner and saw the cage. Ace wanted to burn it down and wished he had grabbed the flamethrower from Daniel.

Rex reached down and felt for the keys. With the fire dying down, it was getting dark quicker.

"You know what I don't understand?" Ace asked.

"What's that?" Rex wondered as he stretched outward, grunting.

"Who caused the explosion?"

"It must have been one of the girls."

I don't know, man. I mean, it was a pretty contained fireball. It only singed the outer limits of the camp. It's almost like it erupted from inside, near the center."

A metallic clink could be heard.

"You got the keys?" Ace asked.

There was a pause.

"Rex?"

"I don't got 'em."

CHAPTER FIVE

It came without warning.

As a guard of the Stalker Clan, he had a specific duty. He had sworn under oath to protect the camp from enemy forces, inside and out. That included Americans, Australians, Thais, Philippines, Southern Vietnamese, and Koreans, as well as escaping prisoners. The man on duty had failed from an unexpected invading force. The creature had claimed him as his first victim. It had slashed his stomach open and planted seeds in his chest. They revived him from his once-thought permanent slumber to use his cells, grow.

A female life form had stopped the evolution. With no other option nearby, the seeds retreated into the body to revive and try again.

Feeling out the grounds, it sensed another was doing the same nearby. Neither life-form could locate the other. One didn't know of its existence while the other was craving his own as well as the intruder's. After a few moments, it grabbed hold of something. It was coppery to the senses, almost like blood. Yet it was no liquid. Instead, the item was shiny and made a sharp, clinking sound. It sounded like there were several pieces attached to a foreign circular ring. There were four appendages of sorts.

It snagged them and the other life-form seemed to stop in his tracks. It heard a muffled sound and then began to investigate. The two men were nervous at the very least. One of them was standing while the other was still on the ground. Both had stopped looking around. It appeared as though they couldn't see in the dark. Neither could the creature, but it could sense their fear was to what they could not see. It deduced that they would have fled had they seen what it had done to the guardsman.

"What is it?" Ace wondered as he scanned the area to no avail. "It's too damn dark! I can't tell!"

Rex remained quiet. He was eerily calm compared to Ace. Both men had seen hard times and were colder inside because of it. When push came to shove though, Ace would break first, but Rex would break harder. If the situation was tense, it would be downright terrifying for Rex.

"We need to get out of here, man!" Ace chattered. He hadn't realized how cold he was. The remaining squad was still naked in the night jungle.

There was suddenly a whipping sound. It was faint but nearby. Ace grabbed Rex by the shoulder and shook him. He felt loose and weak, like he was bound to fall apart at any second. He shook him again and was suddenly grabbed by the hand.

"Rex, what're you doing?!"

"I'm not doing anything!"

Clink clink clink.

Snapping his head forward, Rex turned to the sound of the keys jingling again.

Suddenly, the whole area was bathed in orange. Rex and Ace could see that the guardsman was not only still alive but no more than a few inches from their faces. He had roots and vines sticking out all over.

"Get out of the way!" Daniel shouted.

Rex fell on his rear but managed to scurry off, crab-walking despite the pain. Ace shook his hand hard and was free while pulling the guard's arm with him.

"Fuck!" Ace shouted.

Daniel wasted no time and lit the creature up. It quickly ran around in no particular direction. All it wanted to do was escape the burning sensation. It soon realized there was no way out and fell to its knees where Daniel blasted it with more flames.

Both Ace and Rex turned to their commander who stood there defiantly.

"Let's get out of here," Daniel instructed.

As the three abandoned the keys as well as the creature, Rex began to panic. "How're we getting out of here?"
"We've got weapons, let's blast the lock," Daniel suggested.

"Why didn't we do that in the first place?" Ace wondered.

“I was trying to save our rounds,” Daniel explained. “We don’t know what we’re dealing with out there!”

“But I thought it was dead, that China woman killed it!” Rex said.

“It didn’t look so dead back by the cage.” Daniel looked back over his shoulder. “I’d say it’s spreading itself around.”

Rex began to feel out of his own element. Every bush, every tree was staring at him. The clumps of dirt could have roots sprout out and impale him at any moment. The eerie sense of being watched made him shiver all the way back to the others.

“Alright!” Jemma said. “Let’s get out of here!”

She aimed her AK47 and fired. The first shot was a direct hit, knocking the lock right off the gate. Anton and Ju-ho were ushered out first. Jemma didn’t want to let them out of her sight. Agwa walked by her side, shaking, and broken.

“Here.” Jemma untucked a weapon from her bell bottoms, around her waist. “It’s a souvenir.”

Agwa took the colt commander and cradled it.

“It’s from the departed leader of this camp. Don’t lose it, use it.”

Her sister nodded and a sense of strength and courage came over her once again.

Ju-ho noticed and his face immediately went red. “You killed Se-hun?!”

Jemma didn’t acknowledge her prisoner.

“You killed my brother, bitch?!”

She remained firm in her decision to not engage which enraged the Vietnamese man further.

"If I find out you did this, I'll slit your throat until your head comes off!" Ju-ho snarled.

Anton felt for his scimitar around his belt. It was still there. He knew it was visible for all to see but he also knew that they didn't care. Never bring a blade to a gun fight.

Saber was suddenly struck by a sense of overwhelming internal torture. It felt like his body was getting pulled apart by a cranking machine. Every fiber of his being was in pain, his nerves on fire. After a few spasm-filled seconds he fell to his knees.

Daniel ran to his aid. "Are you alright?" He tried to help his comrade up, but he appeared to weigh more than before, like a ton of bricks. Saber then slowly looked up to his commanding officer. His eyes were glazed over.

"It's happening again!" Daniel shouted.

"We need a medic!" Ace called out to no one in particular.

"Yeah well, the remains of ours are back at that landmine pit!" Vinnie scoffed.

Ace wanted to punch his lights out right then and there. There was no use for him anyway, the man was suffering from P.T.S.D in a fierce way. Still, his oath to work and fight with his brothers in arms kept him at bay.

"He's coming!" Saber said between exasperated gasps.

Agwa ran to Saber's side and she, along with Daniel, managed to get him up. Ace came over to support the man's backside. Rex stayed near in case of further need of assistance.

"Let's get out of here!" Vinnie cried out, annoyed.

"For once, I agree with Vinnie. Let's go before Saber's prophetic vision becomes reality," Daniel stated.

"Visions?" Ace inquired.

He didn't reply.

No one pushed it further, figuring all would be revealed in due time.

The group moved quickly, not worried about stealth at that moment. They were driven by the instinct to survive.

It was unbearable, the constricting pulsing that throbbed with the head injury could not be fathomed. At least there was no real way of telling if the pain was comparable to another's. This was something not experienced in a long time, unprecedented. Yet alive, should be dead, the realization dawned that there had been a second chance given.

Pushing off the dirty ground, memories flashed before more important thoughts such as treating the injury. The first memory to make itself known was of a woman wearing a pink outfit of sorts. She hurt externally and internally. Revenge was of upmost importance. Everything else, the intense pain, the gash, had to wait.

Finally, standing there, another memory came forth. One of lust. No female had been around for a while. She would make a perfect candidate.

Vengeance with a side of defiling. Looking around, weapons strewn about being gripped by cold dead bodies, the best came forth. Hands.

Eddie couldn't believe what his camcorder had picked up. It was unbelievable, a tree-shark-like monster slaughtered a majority of the camp. As he ended the recording, he turned the device off. The reel to reel stopped spinning and the magic ended. Now it was time to call in the bird and get the hell out of there. He didn't sign up for this much horror.

Reaching for the radio to call in the extraction, he realized he couldn't leave yet. There were indeed prisoners in the camp, left behind after a lost war, but those two women were within their group. They needed help. He tucked the Nikon into its respected case, slung the bag over his shoulder, and made his way down the hill he got a clear view of the carnage from. He thought he was handling the decision well until his feet hit the ground. He was overcome with the sense of self preservation. There needed to be some kind of record of what happened here and if he was killed, the footage would be gone, and his legacy forgotten.

The whole operation was bigger than him. It was larger than life. The creature was some kind of government experiment or extraterrestrial. He wondered if it tried mimicking a shark or tree and got messed up in the process. He was sure about one thing: nature had nothing to do with that abomination.

He thought back to the long-haired China woman and felt a stronger feeling than glory, heroism. He had to save them and protect her at all costs. If not and something happened to them, he'd never be able to live with himself. No matter the success, he'd feel he had betrayed them and that was a regret he could not live with. He began to walk in their direction. His feet were killing him with his obese weight pulling him down, but he didn't let it bother him. Instead, he soon found himself tearing through the jungle.

The horror of it all was taking its toll on the mind. Vincent Moretti, once proud boxer of Italy, was now a broken shell of a man. His cowardliness could not be denied as he walked between the two women, hoping they'd be his shields. It was not his usual mindset, self-preservation. Back home he was considered humble and stoic. The toll of being trapped in a prison camp, being fed slop and treated as such, was enough to drive most men mad.

He wanted to be back in his home country and stay at a nice hotel in Rome. The Vietcong were one thing, monsters were another. It was something right out of a story his grandfather would tell him before bed. He had moved to America a mere three years ago and already he was fighting for it. Now everything made even less sense than before.

By his sides, the women didn't even seem to acknowledge him. He was obviously added cargo, but he wasn't sure how Daniel fit into their plan. He had mentioned something about having an idea when he saw the two China women but there was still that connective tissue that was pecking at Vinnie's mind. Never mind the monster, what were these two up to?

"How do you know Commander Stout?" Vinnie asked the older of the two.

"We don't," Jemma stated.

"Then why plan this whole rescue?"

"Because he saved us years ago," Agwa chimed in.

"How's your father doing?" Daniel asked over his shoulder.

The two women paused in place momentarily. "He's dead," Jemma spoke coldly.

Daniel looked down at himself. "I'm sorry to hear that."

"His last dying wish was for us to execute a rescue mission to save you. We owe you and him that much," Jemma explained.

Anton looked at Agwa. "Was it worth getting defiled over?"

Unexpectedly, the timid Agwa spun around and slapped Anton across the face. Jemma then pointed the AK47 at him. He could see the hate in both their eyes and that they wouldn't hesitate to shoot.

Vinnie walked up to Daniel. "Can I have your weapon?"

It was an out-of-nowhere question that took Daniel by surprise. "What?"

"I'm feeling kind of defenseless out here, can I have your flamethrower?"

"Private Moretti, you can have a weapon when you are able to calm yourself in a high stressful situation," Daniel explained.

"Sir, with all due respect, I'm calm now."

"Yeah, because there's nothing stalking us as far as we know," Ace chuckled.

"What do you mean 'as far as we know'?" Vinnie said with air quotes, agitated.

"That things could be anywhere, everywhere. Who knows, maybe giving you a weapon is exactly what it wants us to do. Casualties now would raise its chances of winning this war," Ace said.

"The war is over!" Vinnie cried out.

"And a new one is just beginning," Daniel said, coldly. "Now, let's keep moving."

"I want a weapon!" Vinnie snapped.

"Oh, for fuck's sake," Rex said from the rear of the group. "Let's get a move on! Don't worry, Moretti, I'll protect your panicky fanny."

Vinnie's cheeks blushed red with embarrassment. He was supposed to be a part of an elite death squad and now his comrades were talking down to him. "I could take care of myself alone if I had a weapon."

"Get over it," Ace said. "You should have grabbed one back at the camp instead of hiding behind two women."

Vinnie lunged at Ace but ended up catching the butt of his M1 carbine in the stomach. He fell on his rear hard causing a spasming vibration to shoot up his back. He cried out. "Ah! I think you broke my back!"

“Damnit, can you all just cut it out?!” Jemma shouted. “We need to work together in order to survive this!”

Daniel nodded. “Alright. Whitaker, help Moretti up and shake hands. From now on, no one fights unless it’s against the enemy.” He then turned to the end of the group. “Forbes, that means you too.”

Rex just stood there. He was agitated but willing to cooperate.

Saber noticed how they were starting to come back together, like an actual squad should after a tense situation. They were brothers in arms. It was time they continued acting as such. His connection with the monster may even prove useful. He was surprised no one questioned it too far. He chalked it up to fear. Fear was good, kept them moving. Now they were working together again, it was time to use that frame of mind to see another day.

As Ace helped Vinnie off the ground, the two held each other, hands holding forearms, only seen in brotherly grips or when trying to save another from a fall. They were interlocked but then came apart when some rustling in some nearby brush got their attention. The group backed away slowly.

“Who’s out there?” Ace shouted, still clutching for Vinnie.

Daniel turned to Saber who just stared at the shrubbery. The Filipino didn’t budge, nor did he look all that afraid.

“Commander Stout, what do we do?” Rex spoke up.

“If you saw what we did back at the camp, you’ll know we’re all as good as dead,” Ju-ho chuckled.

"Don't shoot!" came a fatigued voice.

A chubby man donning a steel-plated vest, with a camera around his neck, as well as holding a bag on one shoulder and a satchel on the other came running out of the foliage. He was soaked with sweat and his attire was covered in grime from head to toe.

"Who are you!?" Daniel demanded.

Taking a few deep breaths, the mystery man soon spoke. "My name is Eddie Stokes, I'm a reporter!"

"What're you doing all the way out here in enemy territory?" Daniel wondered.

"As far as I was told there were no more enemies out here!"

"Some reporter," Ace chuckled. "You bleeding-heart liberals seem to think that everything just goes back to normal after a war. I hate to tell you this but you're in the shit!"

"I was an antiwar photographer until I got this scoop about possible POWs being trapped behind enemy lines."

"Let me guess, you felt a little bad and wanted to be a hero. So you got dumped out here by your editor to get a big scoop?" Ace continued to badger the man.

"You're half-right. I'm here to get a scoop, yes. It's on my own accord though. My editor doesn't even know I'm out here."

"So, you're a rebel with a cause?" Rex couldn't help but chuckle.

"No, not a rebel. I still work for the government. Some things just seemed more important than getting a story."

"Like what?" Jemma asked.

Eddie turned to her and blushed. "Saving lives."

There was a pause between them until Vinnie spoke up. "Whatchya got there?"

The reporter followed the soldier's gaze towards his hip. "My revolver?"

"Give it here!" Vinnie smiled greedily.

"I don't think so." Daniel stepped in.

"No?" Vinnie questioned him.

"Yeah, no. I'm willing to help but not to give up my only piece of defense," Eddie explained.

Vinnie stepped forward but Ace pressed his weapon against him. "Want another gut punch, Moretti?"

The soldiers glared at each other for a hot minute before all returned to normal; Vinnie backed off and Ace lowered the gun.

"I have a chopper I can call in. It'll be here if I can get ahold of them within the hour. If not, it'll have to wait until tomorrow," Eddie explained.

"Thank God!" Vinnie cheered.

"Okay, man. Call in the bird!" Rex smiled.

"I need to get to higher ground and away from this camp. The trees are blocking the signal, trust me I already tried. Also, the area's too hot for a pickup. Everything from the fire to the possible Vietcong."

"They're all dead, trust me," Anton stated without emotion.

"Alright, let's get a move on!" Daniel shouted.

It wasn't until the group started moving and Eddie noticed how he was outpacing the soldiers, did he realize how slow their progress would be.

They were there, in that camp, for a long time. Their bodies were shells of their former selves. Yet they still found the urge to carry on. It was both admirable and honorable.

The sight of the bare-butt soldiers didn't escape Eddie either. He looked around and saw a group of four men that were killed by the beast. Their corpses were mostly torn apart but their uniforms remained mostly intact. Like something attacked them from the inside.

"Before we go any further, you men need clothing."

Daniel stopped in place. "He's right."

"There isn't a mall anywhere around here. No clothing store in sight, my friend." Ace said.

Eddie looked down at one of the dead guerrillas.

"No fuckin' way!" Vincent shouted.

"You got a better idea, Vinnie boy?" Rex asked as he made his way over to the freshest stiff he could find.

Against his judgment, the Italian boxing champ fell to his knees and grabbed a heap full of clothing. "They're soaked in blood!"

"We'll stop at a laundromat along the way," Ace chuckled.

Out of all the attained uniforms, Saber managed to get the cleanest attire. It hadn't been savaged by the beast too bad. The original owner most likely perished via swift decapitation judging by the red stains on the shoulders.

Vincent wanted to ask the Filipino if he could trade but managed to think better.

"Alright, let's get a move on," Daniel ordered.

"What about you, Major?" Ace asked his still nude commander.

"I'll be fine," he replied.

No one argued.

"We'll probably find more of these dead goons along the way," Rex chuckled. "One of them is bound to be your size."

CHAPTER SIX

The trek was tricky.

As Daniel had feared, the trails seemed to vanish before their eyes. With the light of the moon and the small flickering at the end of his flamethrower, the absence of light made it difficult for the commander to find his footing let alone lead a group of people through it all. Something within him made him feel that their problems were far from over. The monster back there was riddled with bullets. It had all been too easy.

The humidity of the area was starting to affect most of them. Jemma, Agwa, Saber, and Ju-ho seemed to be adapting to the increase in moisture in the air well. They were used to these climates. Anton, being from snowy Russia, was suffering the worst. Sweat was pouring down his bald head. As perspiration poured, he whipped it out of his eyes, grunting each time. The man couldn't stand it much longer and Daniel half expected him to retaliate, or at the very least complain.

Vinnie too was hot but in a different manner. He seemed rather twitchy. "Moretti, you good?" Daniel asked.

"Yes, sir!" he said through chattering teeth.

"Glad to hear it." Daniel nodded over his shoulder.

Leading the group, he began to guide them closer to the river. Then the accounts of earlier that day hit him. The Vietcong split in two. He began to wonder if that creature could swim. Unlike what Se-hun had said, it looked like the guerrilla had stepped in a trap he had never seen before. Unless there was a razor-sharp thin wire, no stick or blade could cut that clean, that fast.

The nine stood before the flowing water.

"We're going around," Daniel stated.

"What?! Why?!" Eddie asked in a tone louder than he meant.

"Because if you saw what I have seen you wouldn't think twice about avoiding this stream at all costs."

"What happened?" Agwa asked, worriedly.

"I would let Anton or Ju-ho tell you but I don't want anyone even spitting in their direction," Daniel began. "Basically, a man was cut in two as if he were sliced through like butter. I saw a light and then he was in halves. Se-hun said it was a trap. He probably thought it was left behind by our allies. I think it was that creature from earlier. It must've followed us back to the camp."

"Very astute observation," Anton chuckled. "However, you didn't see it attack the camp. It never used light-generated weapons."

Daniel thought about it for a moment. "Regardless, we're going around."

“Need I remind you, Commander, that we need to get to higher ground, out of the brush, in the next thirty-eight minutes,” Eddie stated.

“Then we best get a move on!” Daniel said loud enough for everyone to hear.

“But isn’t the creature dead?” Ju-ho asked.

“Why don’t you take a swim and find out?” Agwa then spat in his direction.

“Oh, I can’t wait to tap your ass again!” Ju-ho chuckled.

Agwa turned in disgust as Jemma guided her away, close to her side.

Enveloping them like the surrounding darkness, the group were swallowed by the jungle once again. Shrouding and concealing, the thick leaves and plants brushed against skin. For Jemma and Agwa, it tickled against their bare stomachs and partially exposed chests. The V-necks on the go go outfits were a nice filtration for airflow, but it made for easy access. Their vigilance was admirable. Eddie saw Jemma almost crack a few times and wanted to aid her any way he could but thought better. Her and her sister had been through enough already. No need to try and make a move to flirt with her.

Noting the AK47 slung over Jemma’s shoulder, he began to try and piece together just what they were doing out there. After coming up with several random scenarios including it being for her own sense of security, he figured he’d just ask. “I take it you’re not prostitutes.”

Jemma only turned slightly at the statement. She then shook her head.

“Then why are you out here with weapons?”

"Because we owe the commander our lives."

"Really, how so?" Eddie said as he fished out a tape recorder. He checked to see if the cassette was in there and then shut the deck and hit record.

Jemma took a deep breath and began. "Our village was raided by a band of pirates in 1958. Me and my family were some of the lucky ones to survive. It is, without a doubt, all thanks to Commander Stout. He handled the operation and saved thirty-eight people that day, that's a little more than half the village. My sister here, Agwa and I almost didn't make it. Commander Stout bull rushed into the heat of combat and carried us to safety."

"What is your name, for public record?" Eddie asked.

"Jemma Reyes. This here is my sister I mentioned before." She nodded to Agwa.

"What does your father think of the rescue mission you two preformed?"

"My father died from a passing bomber while we and our mother went out to the town. He was fixing our mopeds which now lie under the rubble of the camp. Don't ask how the motorbike survived but not my father because I could not tell you. Needless to say, he would be proud of our accomplishment."

"You speak very fluently in English," Eddie stated.

"One has to adapt in the heat of conflict." Jemma smirked.

"I suppose so." Eddie smiled back.

Some time passed before they made it around the river. It was almost dawn, and everyone was exhausted. Boldly, Daniel had remained in front of the group and kept a decent pace throughout their journey. The unfathomable heat made everyone abandon their hopes that it'd be an easy hike. The insurmountable was possible as they moved as one. They barely made sound and their stealth proved useful. There were a handful of times Daniel held up his fist to signify for the group to halt and they did so with ease. Each time was a false alarm but it made everyone more alert.

As the sun's rays spread through the jungle like illuminated rays through a window, the haze set in from the morning dew. The ground was covered in fog. The group found themselves marching through dense shrubbery. Jemma was having a hard time keeping her balance in her platform shoes. She was surprised her sister had more grace than her.

The veil of comfort masking Daniel's face was quickly fading. He didn't like their current predicament. Something felt off. He didn't want to have to stop the group based on a hunch. Instead, he turned and looked back at Anton and Ju-ho who were looking straight ahead. They had no fear on their faces, and it made Daniel question it. They were either aware that the area was safe, or had they accepted their fates? *Were there landmines here?!*

Vroooom.

The loud noise of an engine could be heard as it echoed across the land. Daniel quickly gestured everyone to get down. Ju-ho was having a hard time following that command. He wanted desperately to see one of their trucks out here. He remembered Se-hun had sent them into town to get supplies just a mere hour before the attack. The village center where the markets were was still a far way away. It was conceivable that it would take them until dawn to be on their way almost back.

Daniel turned and saw that Ju-ho was eager and tense, a bad combination. He didn't want to risk the noise of a gunshot drawing attention to the group so he only sat and hoped Ju-ho would remain with them and that his own men wouldn't fire at the runaway target.

A pair of headlights appeared in the dim morning. They were approaching from north-east and barreling through the jungle. It was almost as if they had already spotted them. A terrible feeling sunk in Daniel's gut.

Anton had to hold Ju-ho by the shoulder to keep him in place. "Calm down," he whispered. "In time."

Ju-ho wasn't listening. Instead, Anton's grip tightened which made his hand slip off from his sweaty skin. The young man took off running. As he sprinted across the field, Ace took aim.

"No!" Daniel hoarsely shouted while still trying to keep his voice low.

Thankfully, Ace's reflexes allowed him to process what his commander was saying, and he quickly understood the gravity his implications could have caused. He looked down at himself ashamedly.

The jungle had been alive with sound, chirping, croaking, stridulating. Now it was dead quiet as the truck came into view of the group. In it were four of the Vietcong from Se-hun's Stalker Clan. They were oblivious of the people in front of them in the thick brush. They had not realized that their prisoners were on the run, that their general was dead, and the camp destroyed. As soon as they returned, they had hoped to celebrate with an abundance of alcohol and sharing of the women.

When Ju-ho was seen by the back seat passenger on the driver's side, a few questions crossed his mind. None of them mattered as he screamed for the truck to be stopped.

It came from the bushes right next to Anton. It had been sitting right next to him and he didn't even know it. It looked like a log. Suddenly, it burst forward and charged for Ju-ho. Anton was about to fail his commanding officer and there was nothing he could do about it. The others had been so rigid with fear that no one moved. Now the creature sprung forth and there was no way of stopping it. It seemed to ignore Anton; perhaps it was testing him, holding out to see his capabilities.

Ju-ho would be the one to free them, Anton and he. Maybe he'd even earn some respect from the Russian warlord. He ran out through the brush, into the middle of the road and began waving his arms up and down. From his left, the creature struck. It smashed into him with a force he'd never endured. Not from beatings from his father nor brother. The most uncomfortable feeling of being smothered became all too real as the creature bit into his midsection between his chest and torso, under the armpit, while he was in mid-wave.

The chunk taken out of him was about the size of a frisbee. Flesh clung to him like passengers on a sinking ship, some fell off and away from their host while others held on by a thread. The sinew spun around as blood jetted out in a spray that often sputtered like a hose being stepped on over and over. Gushing forth, Ju-ho vomited heaps of the crimson substance and his mouth tasted coppery. As he drooled red, he still tried to signal the truck and its inhabitants by waving his other arm with barely any success.

Swerving to avoid a head-on collision, the driver turned the wheel hard-right and ended up in a cluster of vines from a nearby tree.

The passenger who first witnessed Ju-ho running from cover was the last to see him alive. As he cried in pain and horror, the creature dug its claws into the wound. Then, with a few hard pulls, Ju-ho was separated into two halves. His upper torso went flying onto the hood of the truck while the lower half fell to the ground in front of the creature.

In that instant, all four of the passengers got their weapons out and began to get out of the vehicle. . . when it suddenly shifted. Veiny vines shot up out of the earth below and through the floor of the truck. They found their targets and imminently went to work, shedding the skin and spreading the seed. All the screams were cut short quickly.

"Burn them!" Vinnie was screaming.

“What?!” Eddie shouted. “Aren’t they dead already?”

“Yes. But now they’re becoming something worse than what they were in their past lives,” Jemma stated.

“What’s that?” Eddie asked.

“Monstrous beasts,” she replied with a stern face.

Daniel quietly yet quickly approached the truck. The creature was just standing on the road, busily munching on Ju-ho. The fire having died out a short while ago, he put the igniter to the tip of the barrel and started the flame. It then shot outward, roaring with the might of a hellish demon. Red hot waves caught, and the truck became engulfed in the fiery substance.

“Commander! Ten o’ clock!” Ace screamed.

The creature had unhooked its jaws from the lower half of the corpse and they were now opening, aiming for Daniel. An impressive spray of light shot out of its mouth. Daniel ducked down just as a beam sliced the truck in front of him. The top came searing off along with the tops of the four heads of the already deceased passengers.

“Fall back!” Daniel shouted.

Everyone ran in multiple directions.

Eddie quickly grabbed Jemma who managed to get ahold of Agwa. The trio sprinted into the jungle while Ace pointed his M1 carbine out and the M4 bayonet stuck the creature from behind.

Daniel was still recovering when Ace jabbed the creature yet again. This time, he twisted the blade a bit to cause extra internal damage. It did little more than to annoy it.

With a swing of its arm, it smacked into the solider who was flung back into the bushes. Rex ran to his aid while Vinnie cowered nearby. Saber had a moment of clarity and realized something was missing. He quickly scanned the area and realized that Anton was gone as were the reporter and the two village women.

"Save yourselves!" Daniel ordered his war-torn men.

"Major! Anton's gone as are the others!" Saber reported.

Daniel was overcome with a sense of duty to protect the civilians whose only crime was of good merit, trying to save them. "Then let's roast this bitch and get the show on the road!" In response, the creature seemed to note the change in attitude. These men did not fear it. Therefore, they would not be so easy to kill.

Saber noticed the creature was observing Rex and Ace and how its stance was of one who was ready to pounce.

"Forbes! Whitaker! Look out!" Saber shouted but it was too late.

Soaring through the air like a hawk detecting a meal, it pinpointed right where to land. Clawed, wooden feet slammed into the muddy earth right behind Ace. Rex fell back in shock.

"Take it!" Ace tossed Rex the M1 carbine.

"No!" As quickly as Rex acquired the weapon, he aimed it at the creature and fired.

The bullet pierced through its head with the force of a stake stabbed into Jell-O, slicing through it like butter. The top half of its head exploded like a water balloon. What remained gurgled and spilled blood, yellow blood. It looked like liquid squash.

It fell down, collapsing atop of Ace. Rex was quick to intervene but only a bit. He managed to get his hand under the creature's chest and then, with Ace's help, the two men hefted it off the downed solider.

"Does somebody wanna tell me what the fuck is going on in this jungle?!" Vinnie screamed.

"I'll be more than happy to," a feminine voice came from over in the brush past the smoldering truck.

CHAPTER SEVEN

An ever-flowing stream.

Trickling down the beaten path, the thin line of liquid babbled as it spilled down the rushing brook. It led to a nearby swamp that was as expansive as it was ominous. It was surrounded by marshland, mostly patches of grass, but there were some boggy sections. When they passed the body of water, there was a thick layer of fog that spread out in a ghostly haze. As they made their way towards a hillside, the mist was evaporating quicker, creating a clearer view of the flora and fauna.

The topography was different. It didn't seem like the jungles of Vietnam anymore but, rather, a forest landscape that stretched for miles with thick trees and wide-open spaces between them. It was an odd juxtaposition from the dense trek the team had been enduring for the past hours.

A plethora of insect life greeted them with open mandibles and proboscises. They bit down onto the soldiers' soft, stretched flesh as their saggy skin hosted a feeding ground for mosquitos the size of a fingernail. The heat was more bearable which caused animals such as deer and even cows to venture up to them.

Daniel was not the leader anymore. The lady ahead of the group, a brunette who introduced herself only by the name of Barbra, was running the show now. It did not relieve Daniel though. He still felt in charge and very responsible for the four remaining members of his squad.

The stream of information he'd soon be receiving worried him so. He knew it was coming and he did not know how much more he could take. Nor his men for that matter. Daniel Stout had been out of the cage more than the others. Even his brother was given that opportunity once they found out they were siblings.

The Vietcong wasted no time torturing the two of them. They brought Ryan down to a begging, fearful boy but they did not break Daniel. He often wondered why Ju-ho shot his brother. Was it some sick sense of revenge because they weren't giving them information themselves?

Suddenly, Barbra stopped. Daniel had been so absorbed in his own thoughts that he hadn't noticed the building in the middle of the forest. He immediately presumed it was because he had a break from always keeping his guard up, but he quickly realized that that wasn't like him. The forest must have been doing something to him, something internally.

"Home sweet home." Barbra smiled with a hint of giddiness.

She opened the doors and the six piled in.

"Barbra! What the actual fuck are you doing?!" a male's voice was heard. "You can't keep running off like this!"

"I'm sorry but they needed help!" Barbra tried to justify herself.

A dark-skinned man came forth. He looked bitter and beaten. His face was filled with rage as his eyes bored into Daniel's. "Who are these men that our trackers have been picking up?"

"POWs. They came from the Stalker Clan's camp," Barbra explained.

"Yes, and we're very weak and tired. Do you have anything to drink or eat?" Vinnie chimed in.

"Great! You rescue them and they want our food," another man could be heard in the room behind the first one.

"Lennie! You've had your fill for today. Give these people some grub!" Barbra insisted.

"The hell with that!" A creaking screech could be heard as the mentioned Lennie got off the furniture. "I don't share."

"We know," the first man said.

"Who might you be?" Daniel asked.

"I'm Roger. I keep this fuckin' place running. Now, who the hell are you all?!"

Daniel went over the introductions. The whole time, Roger didn't take his eyes off Vinnie.

"I don't like this jittery fucker right here."

Vinnie looked at him confusedly. "What's your problem with me?"

"You look like someone who's about to break."

"I'm sure we were all at that point one time or another out here," Daniel tried to calm the man.

"Not me. I'm razor sharp, have been my whole time in this damned jungle."

"It doesn't look like we're in the jungle anymore," Vinnie pushed. "In fact, it looks like a whole new place out there. What the heck are you guys doing here?"

"Let's just calm down. I'll go over it over a bowl of soup," Barbra said.

"We still have people out there," Saber stated.

"He's right. We can't full well leave them to their own devices with those *things* running around out there," Rex said.

"Are they armed?" Roger asked.

Daniel remembered Jemma had an AK47. She gave Agwa a colt commander and Eddie had a revolver. "Somewhat."

"Then they should be fine for now."

"I don't think you understand the gravity of the situation you guys created out there."

"It'll all make sense shortly, Daniel. I promise," Barbra said reassuringly.

"I pray that you're right and that we don't get to them too late."

They sat in the middle of a boardroom-looking section of the building. There was a table in the center and several swivel chairs surrounding it. Behind it all was a projector while, in front, was a pull-down white screen. It was all immediately put to use as the five soldiers sat down, a bit taken aback by the new environment they inhabited.

"Lights, Roger," Barbra told the man.

"Copy, that," Roger said and then flicked off the lights and turned the projector on.

A series of slideshows informed them of the basics. DNA splicing was always brought up though. It soon became a show and tell of intermingling species.

"You see," Barbra began, "it is possible for different species to reproduce together. It's as interesting as same bloodlines creating offspring. Both have abnormal side effects."

"Great, incest. What a way to start a morning," Vinnie chuckled.

Barbra glared at him but paid him no mind.

"As you can see, cats and dogs are most commonly known for inbreeding within their own respective species." Barbra signaled Roger to change to the next slide.

He did so and a picture of a family tree came up with lineage to cats and dogs.

"We get what you're getting at, Misses Scientist Lady," Vinnie said.

"Oh really?" Barbra inquired. "Then what is it your inquisitive mind needs to know about the experiment that we created that you don't already know?"

Vinnie scoffed. "Well, for starters, what exactly is it? Down to the barebones explanation though, please."

Barbra took a deep breath and then sighed. "It's a tree shark."

"I fuckin' knew it!" Rex shouted out. His southern drawl filled up the whole room.

"Okay, and secondly. . . how do we stop them?"

“Wait, them?” Barbra looked confused and concerned all at once. “You already killed it.”

“No, we killed one of them,” Ace added.

“Yeah! They incubate the bodies and breed through them. They create duplicates, goddamned duplicates!” Rex shouted.

Barbra turned to Roger whose dark features became a shade of tan, almost white.

“How?” Barbra tried to speak but, at first, couldn’t find her voice. “How do you know this?”

“We’ve seen it happen a couple of times.” Vinnie shrugged one shoulder as if he had a momentary nerve attack, his ear hitting it.

“How did you stop it?” Roger asked.

“With fire.” Daniel held up his flamethrower.

Barbra’s face went deadpan. “Then we should have burned the truck!”

***

The smoldering corpse of the creature was now nothing but a heap of ash. Anton approached slowly, methodically. He didn’t dare go near the clearly dead animal. There was no telling if it’d spring out at him, ready to attack. A real-life Hollywood jump scare.

Making his way around, he came upon the truck. Vines were pulsating while wrapped around their victims. He began to wonder where the other truck was and why it was taking them so long to get here.

A light gust of wind blew by and swept up the creature in a display of burnt remains that flew in the wind. They covered Anton as he tried to brush them off. He was becoming aggravated by them quickly and began slapping his uniform. His Russian insignia patch almost fell off, but he managed to get the crust off himself.

He then turned back to the truck. The men were unrecognizable save for what was left of their faces. The tops of their heads were gone, coating them in blood. Even their skin was blistered and dry. Suddenly, it was as if they had sucked in gallons of water and were saturated from the inside. The man in the driver's seat's eyes shot open but they weren't normal. They were like two red bulbs, a fleshy circumference.

"Da hell?!"

The driver's hand shot out and snatched onto Anton's. He managed to rip it away before the grip tightened and he held his arm by the wrist. He then slowly backed away. The three passengers then raised their heads slowly in unison. It was like it was staged for a show.

"Zombies!" Anton screeched and then turned to run away.

He ran right into the arms of an able-bodied person. Quickly picking him up to his feet, their eyes met. Anton's darted back and forth as he searched the man's own.

"Se-hun?!"

Se-hun didn't respond. Instead, he looked over Anton's shoulder and saw that the truck door was opening and his undead troops were stepping out.

"What the hell is going on?!" Se-hun wondered, still in a bit of a haze.

"We need to go, sir! Now!"

"Wait, where's Ju-ho!"

"There's no time, sir! We must leave!"

Anton began to run, towing Se-hun behind by the arm. The two men didn't make it more than ten feet before Se-hun tripped over something. He fell to the ground and quickly lifted up his hands. They were covered in blood, his brother's blood. The corpse was mutilated but it clearly was him.

"Ju-ho!"

"We have to go, sir!" Anton stamped his foot which snapped Se-hun out of it.

Collecting themselves, the duo ran into the jungle. The zombies gave chase.

***

Perched against a tree, breathing heavily, Eddie Stokes took a moment to recuperate. Jemma and Agwa were keeping guard while he rested. The two looked like battle-hardened princesses as they scanned the jungle for the enemy.

"Do you think it got them?" Agwa asked her sister.

"I honestly don't know," Jemma said, a hint of fear in her voice.

Eddie noticed this immediately and pushed off the tree. He began walking over to Jemma but restrained himself from holding her. He wanted to comfort her, but he knew his boundaries.

Jemma turned to face him. "Are you all set?"

"I'd like to say yes but I need to check over the equipment," Eddie said as he made his way back over to the supplies he had brought.

Agwa examined the reporter, mainly his gear. She was fascinated with photography and, unlike Jemma, saw the importance of it. "I'll help him."

Jemma didn't take her eyes off the jungle surrounding them.

As Agwa went over and kneeled next to Eddie, he didn't pay her any mind.

"Is that a Nikon?" she asked.

Eddie stopped what he was doing and looked up. "Yes, how do you know . . .?"

"I have a flashbulb camera back at home. I like to receive magazines from passing soldiers about the latest cameras," Agwa explained.

"You like photography?" he asked.

"I admire a good picture."

"There are no bad pictures," Eddie stated.

"Unless the picture's blurred or an object like a finger is in the way, then I agree."

"You know what I mean," he chuckled.

The two sat there in silence for what felt like an eternity.

"Say, does your sister like photography?" Eddie popped the question.

"Why? Trying to find mutual interests?" Agwa smirked.

"If it wasn't so obvious, I'd be more coy." He winked.

Agwa sighed. "Jemma is like a warrior queen. She fights for the right cause. She doesn't like pictures and she hates reporters."

Eddie looked down at himself, visibly upset.

"Maybe you can change that?" Agwa spoke up.

"How?" Eddie's face lit up.

"Prove her wrong, that not all reporters are corrupt."

"Hopefully she'll see that I'm doing this for the right cause much like one she'd fight for."

Agwa nodded in agreement.

"Agwa, Eddie, you guys almost done?" Jemma called from over her shoulder.

"Yes, we're packing up now. Everything looks fine," Agwa shouted.

"Alright, hurry up. I don't want to be here if that thing decides to show up."

The two finished loading the equipment back into the case and satchel. Soon, all three of them were working their way through the thick jungle once more.

***

Barbra could have done anything with her life, been anything. She had the body of a model, the personality of a social butterfly, as well as the brain and hands of a surgeon. Being cooped up with two men who were already at high tension before they were supposed to be evacuated was not how she intended to work.

She, Roger, and Lennie were set to be taken out of the jungle a month ago. The area was compromised, and their chopper taken down by the experiment. Now they dwelled within the old building. None of them knew exactly what it was there for. It did supply the necessities for medical and biological science and was spacious enough to aid in the absence of claustrophobia.

Then came the five men who had death on their heels. It was obvious something horribly wrong was occurring with them and it wasn't just the chase the creature brought about. Barbra had tried to get it out of Daniel profusely, but his mind was too occupied.

"I saw that thing and you must have too!" he shouted. "It nearly missed me with that laser-thing and cut the top of the truck off along with those Vietcong's heads! They're beyond dead."

"Only the tops," Vinnie added.

"We still need to make sure," Barbra insisted.

"I think you're mistaken," Daniel rebutted. "That creature is dead and so are the Vietcong. Meanwhile, I'd like to know those things' capabilities besides the obvious replicative capabilities."

"Yeah, like why it has a freakin' laser." Ace chuckled lightheartedly but with a straight face.

"It's a solar beam, not a laser," Barbra explained.

"Yeah, well. It sure can cut like one," Rex continued. "Hell, I've seen the needle on a record be less precise than that thing. It tore through those scum and that truck like they were melting butter."

"It gathers the light from the sun and is able to expel it from its mouth. Think of it as it giving back to the sun for providing it the ingredients to survive. Feedback, if you will."

"How's this for some feedback!" Vinnie shouted. "If that thing, or one of its clones are still out there, we haven't got a snowballs chance in hell of getting out of here." He glanced down at the flamethrower by Daniel's side.

"You're not getting my weapon, Moretti."

"I know, damnit! The things got to be almost out of fluid anyway." Daniel picked it up and gave it a once over. "She's still got a bit of juice left in 'er."

"Not enough as far as I'm concerned!" Vinnie cried out.

"Aren't we forgetting something?" Saber stated. "The others are still out there. Moretti, if you think *we* barely have a chance, then what kind of chance do they have?!"

"The flamethrower seems to be the only successful weapon against the. . . tree shark. There's got to be a better name for it." Daniel turned to Barbra.

"I call her Thorn," Barbra stated.

"Well, that's fitting. She's a real thorn in all of our sides!" Vinnie scoffed.

"Look, guys!" Roger spoke up from behind the projector. "If you want to save your friends, I suggest we get a move on. It'll be getting much hotter soon and it'll be easier the earlier we get this done."

"Let's go, men!" Daniel said.

"Wait!" Barbra shouted. "We need a plan of escape. I suggest that, now that we have some extra man and fire power, we can make the best of the situation."

"How so?" Daniel asked.

"Roger, you take Saber here and Lennie and head to the boat. Gather what you can here. Only necessary items. The more flammable the better. Then bring the boat around to the coastline. We'll meet you there."

"Copy that," Roger said and then began out the door.

"Commander." Saber turned to Daniel.

"It's alright. You're too weak to help us in this battle but you can still guard them and save all of us."

Saber thought about it briefly. "Yes sir."

The five men corralled around each other and huddled in close.

"We are the beasts of the jungle!" Daniel shouted.

"Hoorah!" the four replied in unison.

"We're the enemy they can't see, that they can't sneak up on!"

"Hoorah!"

"Men, we're going to get through this and, once we do, we'll go home!"

"Hoo-fuckin'-rah!" they all said as if reading each other's minds.

"I need someone who is good with electronics," Barbra inquired.

Rex stepped up. "I'm your guy."

"If we can get a distress call out it'd be all the better!"

"Forget it!" Lennie said as he entered the meeting room.

It was the first time the squad had seen him, and he lived up to his description. He was obese, even more so than Eddie. His stomach was hanging out of his white tank top which was covered with stains.

"Why?" Rex asked.

"I've tried fixing that contraption for a couple of weeks now. It's shot."

"To be fair, tubby, I can probably fit in the hard-to-reach places better." Rex smirked.

Lennie mock laughed. "Have fun."

"Alright, let's haul ass and move out!" Daniel commanded with the upmost authority.

Barbra and Rex headed up to the communications room on the second floor while Saber, Roger, and Lennie got into an old four-wheeler and sped off down the forest path. Meanwhile, Daniel, Ace, and Vinnie headed off towards the jungle, the way they came had come.

CHAPTER EIGHT

It gave life.

A tumor nature would have trouble shaking, the specimen spread its seed across the open pasture. It was once a farming village but now, it remained with dilapidated huts and dead weeds instead of a lush landscape. No life had grown on the land for half a year, but it was slowly beginning to see vegetation.

Then the intruder came. The spores of eggs ejaculated onto the jungle floor were slow-acting toxins to the environment. They fed on the dirt and absorbed the sun. The open area provided enough of both of these things to sustain their lives.

After some time, the host died. It had barely lived with the injuries it had incurred. The last act of survival was species propagation asexually. What started as three hundred seeds turned into dozens of throbbing egg sacks. Soon it would whittle down to less than ten. The most born at one time was three. Each had amassed such an energy that they were borderline oak.

Processes like these normally took a prolonged amount of time. Things had to be perfect for the offspring to mature. These eggs would grow remarkably fast and the organism within would begin to form within a few minutes.

The first identifying trait was the wooden dorsal fin.

Then they became one.

***

The murky green water of the swamp seemed fitting for the topography. Coated in slimy Eucheuma seaweed and grass growth that stuck high out of the water and danced around like waving fingers, beckoning for visitors to enter, the lagoon was most uninviting. Lennie half expected a bog beast to burst from within and grab him as they neared the location.

Saturated in mud, the trail to get to the tugboat was a slippery one. Lennie and Roger both nearly slipped and fell several times. Saber seemed to adjust just fine. As they got to the dock, Saber in the lead, the man seemingly unfazed by anything, he held up his arm.

"What is it?" Lennie asked with bated breath.

In truth, Lennie didn't want to have to be a part of any mission. He was too tired and sore all the time and the sweltering heat was killing him daily. Though he masked it well, he would much rather lay low and not get in the way.

Saber didn't respond to the out-of-shape technician. Instead, he scanned the surrounding jungle. In truth, he didn't pick up any bogies. Sound echoed throughout the vicinity which was, as far as Saber was concerned, a relief. He then waved the two men to approach the dock with him.

"Alright, let's get this shit aboard and get to work!" Roger said as he unslung the backpack from his shoulders.

In it were a couple of M-16s and a grenade. As Saber situated the weapons on the boat, Lennie attempted to climb over the gunwale. He was struggling so Roger had to help him. Once the two men were aboard, they got to work on the engine.

Saber began to walk away.

"Hey, man! Where are you going!?" Roger exclaimed.

"I need to get to a higher vantage point. I'm going to be up on that hill over there." He pointed.

"If you see anything, just holler," Lennie pleaded.

It was not the best idea to give away his position but, if the perfect opportunity arose to do so, he'd do it. He nodded in response and trudged up the muddy trail.

***

"We'll be out in the open! Defenseless!" Vinnie practically screamed.

"Listen, I don't love it any more than you do. However, this may be the quickest path to get back to the road and pick up tracks on Eddie and the girls," Daniel explained.

"Well, I'll just hang back here and keep guard," Vinnie said nonchalantly.

"The hell you will!" Ace shouted. "You've been too neglectful of your duties already. We need to stick together and finish this."

"What do you know about duty?! You're just as scared as I am. When push comes to shove, you'd be the first to toss the sickly." Vinnie's mental health was waning.

Suddenly, Ace's body slammed into Vinnie's. He pinned him to the ground, saliva drooling from his sneering lips. "You're not sick! Just a selfish, cowardly motherfucker!"

"I am not!" Vinnie tried to get out from under Ace, but it was no good.

"Unless you're forgetting, I have a sick mother at home. My aunt won't stick around after she's gone, and my brother will be all alone. My *kid* brother!"

"We've all got shit to clear up back home!" Vinnie cried out.

"Of course we do! And if we want to get back there, I suggest we all work together!" Ace was screaming now.

"Get off me, man!" Vinnie winced in pain as Ace's palms dug into his shoulders.

Daniel managed to get a handle on Ace and lift him from under his armpits. "Will you two knock it off! You're not acting like brothers in arms! You're both acting like brothers at length!"

Ace shook himself free from his commanding officer. "What's this brother's thing? You keep bringing it up! Hell, I've sensed that you've thought about it every time we fought together!"

"We are a death squad. We have to rely on each other in order to survive and succeed. Right now, I'm not seeing that."

"Brothers can be independent of each other," Ace snarled.

"Is that what you want to be? Alone, fighting an army?!"

"If it gets me back to my real brother then yes." Ace turned to Vinnie who was still on the ground. "I don't need anyone hampering that for me."

He then gathered his M1 carbine and looked at Daniel with seething eyes. "Let's get this over with!"

***

Rex examined the communications room as he entered through its door. It was rudimentary at the very least. There was a radio with a microphone attached. The knobs were all set to the right frequency according to Barbra. It was as simple as a two-way radio. They just needed to reach someone on the other end.

"I'll see what I can do," he told her.

"Don't mess with the knobs." Rex turned to her and she shrugged. "We almost got through one time on that station, but it cut out."

He then went over and sat in the swivel chair. As he spun around, something caught his eye. It was a small compartment located next to the desk close to the floor. "What's down there?"

"We thought it was an outlet," she said, confusedly.

Looking over the cords, he didn't see any that directly lined up with the ones that were attached to it. He examined further and noticed another outlet practically invisible to the naked eye. It was stuck to the inside of the desk with a glue of sorts. He tried to grab it to see if it was loose, but it was stuck on like cement.

"What's this?"

Barbra leaned forward and tried to see what he was talking about. She couldn't get a clear view. "I don't see it."

"Right where my hand is," he stated.

She got closer and saw up to his wrist. "I still can't see it."

"It looks like an outlet of sorts. It's not loose but I think one of the cables is supposed to attach to it."

He fished around for any loose cables on the floor with his other hand, his rear supporting his back and holding him up. After a solid minute he couldn't locate anything. He then decided to feel for any that might be near the device. It was there, right in front of it. He picked up the cord and plugged it in.

The bass guitar of a tune kicked on. Rex immediately recognized the song was *We Gotta Get Out of This Place* by The Animals. He loved the song. He instantly missed his tape player.

"Well, that's the radio."

"Will that help?" Barbra asked, clearly clueless.

"Let's find out."

Smash.

An appendage, clearly wooden in genetic make-up, came crashing through the wall. The cords became tangled and unplugged from everything, the radio crashed onto the ground, dragging the microphone with it. The song still played.

Barbra gave a shrill scream as the tree shark began to climb into the room. Rex quickly tried to assess the situation by looking for a weapon. Any weapon. As this happened, the chorus kicked in. Eric Burdon's vocals screamed in response after every verse.

Placing one foot in the room, the other soon followed, the creature looked around. It watched Rex with supreme interest. Barbra was an easier target, but he posed a threat.

Rex wished the others had left them a weapon. He knew Daniel figured they'd be safe in the secure room. They all underestimated the strength of their enemy. Without much choice, he grabbed the microphone and charged at the creature.

One swing, one hit, it stumbled backwards. It righted itself faster than Rex could get a second swing in. Grabbing the soldier by the wrist, it snapped his whole arm backwards. His bone broke through skin as blood poured out in a steady stream.

"Ahhh, son of a bitch!" he screamed.

Barbra began to cower towards the corner.

Rex turned to her. "Get the fuck out of here!" He swung his other arm and landed a hit in the thing's face. His hand immediately swelled up. As far as Rex was concerned, he was not out of commission yet. He lifted himself upward and kicked the creature in the chest, sending both he and it spiraling backward in different directions.

The scientist quicky rushed to his aid. "Get up,
oldier!"

He went to put his right hand down for support but fell face-first onto the floor instead. Looking down, the grim realization came over him. His arm was gone, separated at the elbow.

"Oh Jesus!" he cried out.

A stabbing pain shot through his leg as something dug into his Achilles heel. Stick-like claws were jammed in there. They dragged Rex across the floor and closer to the waiting jaws of the tree shark.

"No!" both Rex and Barbra shouted in unison.

The mighty maw opened, and he was stuffed in its mouth. Chomping down, chewing on flesh and bone, the creature wasted no time consuming the solider. Soon, he was gone, entirely eaten.

Barbra spun around and ran for the door. She slammed right into a hulking figure. It was a second tree shark. It stormed towards her. "Please forgive me!"

Her creation reached out for her. "God, forgive me!"

Before it could get ahold of her, the first tree shark, with arms extended outward, brought its hands forward in a massive clapping motion. Her head popped like a zit. Chunks of brain matter and skull bone sprayed everywhere.

There was no better life for them as the song came to an end.

***

"I think we're high enough," Eddie stated as he surveyed the surrounding area.

"Alright then, make the call!" Jemma demanded.

Wasting no time, he pulled his radio out from one of his Velcro pockets. Keeping it to the same frequency was hard enough but he had managed to remember most of the station numbers in case something got turned.

He turned it on. After holding it up to the sky for a few seconds, fully expecting static, he was surprised to hear nothing. The radio waves were most likely clear. He quickly brought the communication equipment to his face and began. "Mayday! Mayday! Mayday! This is Stokes calling brown eagle one, Stokes calling brown eagle one. I and several others need a rescue pick up A.S.A.P, over."

For a few minutes there wasn't a response as he relayed the message twice more. Then, static began to fill the dead air. "I repeat, we have a situation and need immediate extraction. Can you pick us up from the beach on the north-east side of the prison camp? We're approximately two clicks from that general vicinity, over."

A gargled voice emitted from the device. There was too much amplification and noise to make it out.

"Can you repeat that? Is that you, brown eagle?"

The other end of the line began to make a strange sound. It was almost like screaming. It was distorted to the point that it sounded otherworldly. The screech turned to almost banshee levels of sound and Eddie dropped the radio to cover his ears, as did the women.

It kept growing and growing in intensity.

Agwa instinctively reached down, grabbed the radio, and tossed it down the rocky hill where it smashed on a boulder.

"Why did you do that?!" Eddie cried out.

"They weren't going to help us!" Agwa argued.

"Then we're stuck here unless the others found a way to communicate with the outside world!" Eddie shouted out of anger at the situation.

Jemma didn't see it that way. "Don't yell at my sister!"

"Jemma, it's alright."

"The hell it is! We need to work together to get out of here and not shout like five-year-olds," her sister argued.

"She's right. I apologize," Eddie said softly.

Jemma looked at him, angry still. "I don't think you know the shitstorm you walked into even before this monster started chasing us."

"What do you mean?"

"You reporters are all the same. If you did, in fact, find the POWs at that prison camp, would you have done anything about it or just snapped pictures?"

"No!" Eddie screamed.

"No?" Jemma asked.

"No, I wouldn't have just snapped damned pictures. I would have done something!"

"Like what? Take on the whole camp with your revolver?"

"I'm not a war-hero," Eddie argued.

"Clearly."

"I would have called in for help!"

"I can see that." She gave him a once over with her eyes.

"I may be overweight and clumsy, but I still managed to see you two well before we were improperly introduced."

"What are you talking about?" Jemma wondered.

"I saw you and your sister on your mopeds. I thought you were the Vietcong, so I hid behind some bushes." Eddie sighed and then continued. "I also saw that you were heading in the direction of the camp. I vowed to protect you by any means necessary. Thankfully, I didn't have to during my trek to the prison camp. However, I would've laid down my life for you, both of you."

"Why?" Jemma demanded to know.

"Because I may not be a hero, but I am a good man who knows right from wrong. Hell, the reason they even dropped me off here was because I thought this was an interesting idea for a story and no other reporter back at the office had the balls to do it. They feared for their own lives. Not me though. I'm here to prove to the world that we're not all bloodsuckers," Eddie stated.

There was a momentary silence.

"It sounds like you've convinced yourself of that. Now prove it to us," Jemma said.

"Huh?" Eddie inquired.

"If the time comes, show the truth in your words," Jemma told him.

She then brushed past him and went down the hill.

"It seems to me like you're on the right track." Agwa smiled.

Eddie gave a reassuring smile. "You both have my word and it's worth a lot."

"*Stokes, is that you, over?*" A voice came from where the radio lay.

They were almost out of earshot by the time the receiver of the call responded. Eddie ran towards the rocks and gently picked up the delicate remains of the radio. "Brown eagle, this is Stokes! We need a pick up! Meet us northeast on the beach we passed on the way in. We'll be there within the next couple of hours, over!"

There was silence for a brief moment. Then the voice came back on. "*Roger, pick up time in two hours, northeast on beach, over.*"

"Yes! Thank you! We'll be there! Over and out!" Eddie tried to tuck the radio back into his pocket, but it crumpled before his very eyes.

"We need to get a move on. Once the chopper collects us, we'll circle back for the others," Eddie told Jemma and Agwa, who had just approached.

"Let's not waste time," Jemma said with a bit more optimism in her voice.

The three then made their way back into the jungle.

CHAPTER NINE

"They're spreading!"

Anton, the merciless merc, was not intimidated easily. He preferred the fear of others to boost his egotistical persona. Now, seeing the Vietcong reduced to husks of their former selves and still coming back as zombified organisms with plant-like features was unfathomable. He could only imagine what was coursing through them to bring their corrosive corpses back from the dead.

Spittle spilled from their snarling lips as the results of a creature unknown to this earthly plane marched through the jungle. They had no control over their minds. Their memories, a dark dream sent spiraling into forbidden levels of their subconscious. They had no intellectual thought but instead acted in a hive mind. Their leader was the oldest specimen. After it perished, the next elder would take its place. There were no kings or queens, only ranks by species and age.

Se-hun saw them trudging past them as he and Anton hid down a slightly steep hillside with trees that covered their hiding spot. To him, they were more than just hulking brutes. They were experiments that could be collected and controlled. "We need them."

"The hell we do!" Anton whispered hoarsely. "We need to get out of here is more like it."

"Get a grip. There is a time and place to be a coward, and this isn't either."

"Cowardice and survival are the same thing in this case as far as I'm concerned," Anton retorted.

"You want to run? Go for it. You won't make it fifteen feet without me."

"Oh really?" Anton said in a mocking tone.

"I know this jungle like the back of my hand. Every twig, every branch, every leaf. It's all mine and I know it. Now, unless you want to die, you'll do exactly as I say." There was no emotion in Se-hun's voice.

His partner thought it over. "What do you suggest?"

Se-hun shifted his upper lip. "I suggest we find where those pathetic Americans ran off to and terminate them. Then we can figure out how to capture these things."

"Why do you care about them?"

"Don't you want to take out their leader?" Anton looked down at himself. Se-hun quickly noticed. "Ah, I see. I know you too well. I know you've been meaning to scrape that American pig off your boot ever since he arrived."

"I have my reason."

"And what reason is that?"

Again, Anton pondered on what the man said. "He makes me feel like a fool. No one gets to do that."

"Oh, and why does he make you feel like a fool?"

"Because he doesn't fear me. Everyone should fear me." Anton looked to where the zombies were wandering off to. "I want to cut the fear from him and eat it."

"How do we find them?"

Anton turned back to Se-hun with an insidious grin. "I have an idea."

***

"It's a fuckin' dead end!" Vinnie shouted.

Out in the field was nothing but crops of plants and an abundance of tall grass. It was thick all around with limited visibility. The further they went in, the higher the grass towered over them. It practically loomed over them at this point.

"Guys, it's getting tight. I suggest we head back," Ace stated.

"Yeah, if we can even find our way back!" Vinnie said while panting.

"Don't give up on us now, Moretti!" Daniel snapped his head in his direction.

Vinnie paced back and forth while still keeping his comrades in his line-of-sight. He was starting to doubt his commanding officer. They had been through so much only to end up lost. "We're in the garden of hell, you know?!"

"Right, and I'm the angel who's going to save your sorry ass," Ace chuckled.

There was no time to laugh at his snarky remark. Instead, Vinnie could only scream as a ghoulish humanoid jumped atop Ace.

“Oh shit!” Vinnie screamed.

“Get it off of me!” Ace shouted as he whipped his body back and forth.

The mangled man tried to bite down on his neck, but the constant shifting made his head snap back and forth. The popping and creaking of bones could be heard as he practically wiggled in place.

Ace managed to get a good grip on the top of the zombie’s head and flung him over his shoulders and onto the ground. He then noticed the exposed skull; there was a thin layer that kept the brain from falling out.

Daniel quickly aimed the flamethrower at him and doused him in flames. Writhing with agonized screeches to accompany the dance of the dead, he finally collapsed, pieces of flesh melting away in chunky bits.

More moans could be heard. The three men turned and saw shimmying corpses charging towards them.

“Fall back!” Daniel shouted.

“To where?!” Vinnie asked.

It was a genuine question. Still, he had to give an answer. “Just turn around and run!” Daniel screamed.

***

It appeared as though they were just turning random knobs and connecting certain wires. Saber wasn’t too familiar with boats, but he didn’t expect it to take this long to get it started up. Nevertheless, Roger and Lennie had spent almost half an hour on the dinky, dingy vessel and it seemed they were getting nowhere.

Saber had been sitting in the same position, kneeling forward on one knee with the other supporting his weight, the whole time. He would never complain about discomfort. Annoyance was different though and he was close to calling the whole thing off.

"This dump-bucket might as well be a toilet," Lennie shouted. "The grooves are filled with gunk, the engine has seaweed tangled in it, and I don't know if you noticed, but there are moss stains on the hull."

"Will you quit it!" Roger snapped back. "And, for your information, she *did* have seaweed in the engine."

He pulled up a clunk of the goopy substance and then dropped it overboard. "Give it another rev."

"Okay, but just one more time."

"Humor me." Roger smirked.

Lennie walked over with as much enthusiasm as Saber looked at them with. The two locked eyes, both inwardly praying but not hoping for much. Maybe a gurgle or even a spout of water shooting out. Lennie turned the key in the ignition, and it roared to life.

"Fuck yeah!" Roger exclaimed.

Saber sighed with relief. "Alright, meet us at the beach."

"You ain't comin' with us?!" Lennie called out.

"I have to make sure my brothers are alright. Something akin to civic responsibility, if you will," Saber explained.

"Alright, we'll meet you at the northeast end. Be there in the next hour or so or we'll come to the shore to find you. Please don't make us do that," Roger said with a stern expression.

Saber nodded and began into the jungle.

Roger reached for the radio. "I doubt it'll work beyond static. Maybe we can get some tunes even."

"Look who's letting loose," Lennie chuckled.

After fidgeting with the knobs and antennas for a few minutes, he managed to get a radio station. *Gimmie Shelter* by The Rolling Stones came on. It was right near the beginning of the song.

The bluesy jam echoed through the swamp with the scraping of the guiro in the background accentuating the rather Cajun experience. Mick Jagger's vocals came on and began to bring the song to life but when Merry Clayton came on, it seemed to breathe new energy into the tune.

Both Roger and Lennie were lost in the song and their surroundings. No number of mosquitoes or amount of humidity could drag them from the importance of it all.

"I think I'm going to miss this place," Lennie finally said.

Roger gave a hearty laugh.

"What's so funny?" Lennie asked.

"I was expecting the opposite from you to be honest."

"Come on, you're seriously not going to miss this freedom?" He spread his hands outward.

"This isn't a free place, Leonard. It's a place of deceptive hate."

"Not all of it. There is just enough room for innocence in all this betrayal and blind rage."

Roger smiled. "Maybe someday."

Suddenly, during the song, Merry Clayton's voice broke. It made Lennie's toes curl. It was such a powerful song with deep lyrics accompanied by strong performances. Despite that, it was catchy, a real head bopping, foot tapping good time.

Unbeknownst to Roger, Lennie saw his head swaying back and forth as the song progressed to its aggressive climax.

Saber made his way back to the road. The four-wheeler should still be there. The trek was harder on the way back going uphill. Still, he was alert. No signs of enemy forces were prevalent. There was still an uneasiness in the air though.

When he got back to the road, a sense of urgency came over him. He wanted to get out of there faster than his two legs could possibly take him.

Slowly swinging one sore leg over the vehicle, he produced the keys and placed them in the ignition. As he drove off, he checked his gages. He only had enough gas to go a couple more miles.

He sighed. *If things hadn't been hard enough already.*

***

As the smoke began to clear, a hulking heap of parts emerged through it. The engine was slowly giving out and the muffler was of no use. The whole truck rattled and coughed as it pressed on. There were no signs of it being reparable in these conditions.

The four occupants knew their leader would be aggravated. That concern quicky faded once they saw the state of the other truck.

Plant life caused a confusing network of roots and vines that crisscrossed and were tangled yet somehow all led to the same source. One of the men got out of the truck. He inched closer and closer and the more he saw, the more he was concerned.

"It looks like the vines are dead."

"Chau, what are you saying?"

"I'm saying that whatever this plant was attached to seemed to give life to it. Now that it's gone, they've served their purpose."

"Okay, I may be no plant expert but don't flowers or trees usually come from stuff like this?" the Vietcong wondered.

"It's almost as if it is a reverse life cycle for a plant. The finished product feeds its vines to a host, maybe even planting seeds inside."

"That's all well and good but where are the men that were inside?" the driver asked.

"I don't know, Lam." Chau was about to continue when some rustling could be heard from the brush.

The backseat passengers got out of the truck, as did Lam. Chau quickly joined their sides.

"I'm giving whoever's out there three seconds to come out or we'll open fire," Lam instructed.

He didn't even get to the count of one when a chubby man decked out in gear emerged from the bushes.

"Don't shoot!" Eddie begged.

"Who are you?!" Lam inquired.

Eddie slowly reached down and held up his camera. "Photographer."

"What do you take pictures of fat man?" Lam asked.

"Uh, trees," Eddie said while averting his gaze.

"Look at me when you talk to me," Lam demanded.

Eddie focused on him.

"If you can tell me what happened here, I'll go easy on you," Lam offered.

"Do I have a choice?" Eddie gave a slight smirk.

The Vietcong all shook their heads in unison.

Taking a deep breath, he began. "There's a monster out here. It came from the jungle and tore apart your men with vines. As to where your men are now, I can't say because I have no idea."

"Monster?" Chau asked, perplexedly.

"It's like nothing I have ever seen before."

"If you could describe it?" Chau pressed, pushing up his glasses closer to his eyes.

"It was like, um, a shark."

"A shark?!" Lam bellowed with laughter.

"A shark made of bark and wood. It can use the jungle as its own weapon."

"I've heard enough. Get him into the car. We'll get what we want out of him back at the camp," Lam instructed.

"The camp is destroyed!" Eddie exclaimed.

The Vietcong stopped dead in their tracks.

"What did you say?" Lam asked, his short temper rising.

A bullet clipped his ear. It sent it flying off somewhere on the dirt road. "Ah! Son of a bitch!" Lam screamed.

Jemma and Agwa ran out of the brush. They stood by Eddie's side.

Between the throbbing pain and blood pulsating from where his ear used to be, Lam noticed the younger woman holding a familiar weapon. "Where did you get that?!" he asked between gritted teeth.

"Don't worry," Agwa said. "He won't be needing it anymore."

"That colt commander belongs to Se-hun!" one of the other Vietcong shouted.

"No shit!" Lam said as he breathed hard, and spittle shot through his teeth. He was practically foaming at the mouth.

Eddie, Jemma, and Agwa began to back away into the jungle. The four Vietcong stared them down. Soon, the civilians were hidden amongst the trees.

"Should we go after them?!" Chau asked.

Lam looked back at the truck. "Yes, but we'll go in style."

***

Pushing further through the tall grass, Daniel led Vinnie and Ace towards hopeful freedom from the green hell. There had been no signs of openings since the run-in with the reanimated Vietcong soldiers. The sandy earth made it hard on their feet to run. Vinnie and Ace had the wrong boot size from the attire they took from the soldiers. They were either one size too big or too small.

Vinnie was beginning to hyperventilate. He didn't want to die out here from some shark zombies. There was too much to do back home. Too many fights in the ring to enact.

Ace was lagging a bit. The boots kept him behind his comrades. He was a size ten but the footwear he was donning were a size eight and a half. His heel barely touched down on the bottom causing the boots to flop around a bit when he ran.

Daniel looked back at the two just in time to see one of the undead ghouls leap forward and jump down on Ace. The soldier's M1 carbine went flying from his hand. He stopped dead in his tracks and aimed the flamethrower. The first chance he would have with Ace out of the way, he would douse the zombified Vietcong in a hot orange embrace.

"Moretti, help him!" Daniel shouted.

Vinnie didn't stop running. He kept on until he was near his commanding officer.

"Moretti!" Daniel reached out and grabbed his arm. "Help Whitaker!"

With a quick glance over his shoulder, Vinnie saw his brother in arms pinned down by one of the zombies. The other two were closing in.

"I, I don't know. . . "

"Snap out of it, damnit!" Daniel shouted.

Vinnie was having trouble focusing. His mind was going a million miles per minute. Part of him wanted him to abandon them and save himself. The slightly more dominant side brought him back to the days in training and even in the prison camp. They had all been through hell twice. They weren't out of the jungle yet. He so badly wanted to help but realized that there was nothing he could do. If he pushed the zombie off it might get up and attack him.

The only plan of attack that might work would be to bull rush the zombie. He just hoped he was quicker to recover and get back to the others.

Readying his stance, he began to charge. He let out a primal yell. The other two zombies challenged him with massive roars. They were hauntingly bone-chilling enough to stop Vinnie in his tracks. He used whatever energy he had left and ducked into the long grass.

"Fucking coward!" Daniel screamed.

He then put his M2 flamethrower down and unslung the backpack from himself. He then ran forward and grabbed Ace's M1 carbine and then stuck the zombie atop Ace in the head with the bayonet. It was protruding out the other side. Daniel gave it a strong yank, but it wouldn't come free.

The zombie wasn't dead. It was drooling yellow goop from its mouth and blood was pumping out of both sides of its head. Yet it refused to go down. Daniel lined up his shot the best he could and fired. The report was hard enough to knock Daniel's frail body back. The top of the zombie's head was blown off. It released its grip from Ace who poorly crab-walked out from underneath it, barely able to push himself up on all fours.

Daniel handed the weapon back to Ace who took it and put a few more rounds into the corpse. The two then began to back away from the encroaching zombies.

"Have we got this, Commander?" Ace asked.

"You bet, buddy," Daniel said as he ran over and reached for his M2 flamethrower, and the tanks of fuel attached to the back-strap.

A wooden foot came down and crushed the weapon. Daniel was only five feet away. Ace turned back and saw the tree shark was standing there, its wooden teeth slowly opening and closing. It was as if it were inviting them in.

Quick to recover, Daniel back walked towards Ace who was smirking. "Tree shark to the left, zombies to the right, and here I am stuck in the middle with you."

"No time to semi-quote a Stealers Wheel song!" Daniel shouted.

The zombies were closer so Ace aimed at them.

"No!" Daniel shouted.

"What?!" Ace questioned.

"Aim for the fuel tanks."

Ace followed Daniel's gaze and saw the two tanks secured to the backpack. He then aimed his weapon. "I hope you didn't need anything in there."

He was about to fire when a pair of wooden hands reached out from the grass behind him and grabbed him by the shoulders. They pulled him back. Before Daniel realized what had happened, there was a sickening crunching sound. When he looked back he saw that another tree shark was there with its jaws clamped over the top of Ace's head.

"Take it!" Ace cried out as he handed his friend the M1 carbine.

Applying more pressure, the tree shark bit down harder and the top of Ace's head ripped off with a sickening wet, crackling sound. His arms fell to his sides and jelly-like brains fell from his open cranium.

"No!" Daniel screamed.

He spun back around and fired at the fuel tanks. A ball of flame erupted, and a wave of air pushed the tall grass down. Daniel got a glimpse over the grass and saw how close he was to the facility. It was nearly a hundred yards away.

CHAPTER TEN

Eruption.

Both Se-hun and Anton saw the explosion in the field as well as the complex behind it. As the fire spread, it became more visible, as did the creatures within the brush. There were two zombies and a tree shark as well as a man still standing and another dead in a heap of gore. The plant fish monstrosity was engulfed in flames as one of the zombified infected began to retreat towards the building.

Se-hun knew that the men who were once under his command were now unthinking, untrainable, and undead. It seemed he only had Anton to turn to now for support and that was up for debate.

"Did my brother become one of those things?" Se-hun said coldly.

"No." Anton was statuesque. "His fate was arguably quicker than the men who were turned into those mindless monsters." They stood in silence.

"Anton, I told you to look after him. Now, not only is my younger brother dead, but my camp is destroyed, my men are either dead or undead, and all I have is you."

"What are you saying, Se-hun?"

"I'm saying that it's awfully convenient, is all."

"You would find that a suitable excuse. I tried to protect Ju-ho, but fate was faster than my bullets."

"I hope you are telling me the truth. For your sake."

"I am," Anton snarled.

"Regardless, we still need to start over."

"Start over?!" Anton looked perplexed.

"We'll rally up some villagers and train them. We'll be up and operational again within a year."

"You will not be getting Russian support on your next escapade."

"What do you mean?"

Anton smirked. "After my superiors find out that your camp was destroyed and your prisoners escaped as well as all your men gone, it won't be looked upon with mercy."

"Then we'll just have to get them back."

"Well, it looks like one's heading to that facility as we stand here discussing the future."

Se-hun narrowed his eyes and looked across the field. "Stout."

"He's still alive and he's mine. Besides. We could get more support if we capture, oh say, a reporter."

"A reporter?"

"Yes, we gained some intel when one of my scouts surveyed the area twenty-two hours ago. Apparently, a helicopter dropped off a passenger in the middle of the jungle. Satellites picked up an image of him. He was armed with a camera, a case that presumably had a camcorder in it, given the Nikon symbol, and a map."

"When were you going to tell me of him?!" Se-hun shouted.

"When your men captured him. He carried a small piece, a revolver. No big deal. Plus, it'd be an easier catch if he came to us rather than they chase after him."

"Sounds like your support is much more valuable than I initially thought."

"If you can acquire this reporter, I'll make sure to put in a good word for you back with the KGB."

"If he's not a reporter?"

"Then he's an adrenaline junkie with a camera. Either way he's American."

"Alright, I'm assuming he's helping the POWs. We get Daniel and the others, and we'll more than likely be able to snag him on the way back."

"Back to what? The camp is destroyed."

"Base camp is gone, yes, but I have several others littered around the jungle. Each with enough men to make up a platoon."

"I guess we both have secrets."

"And now that they're out in the open, let's finish this."

***

Eddie saw the fireball. Jemma and Agwa felt the tremor below them shortly after. At first, there were no words spoken between them. They stood in stoic silence. It was as if they were trying to read each other's minds, maybe figure out the next course of action.

The rumbling sound of the explosion was dying down. It was becoming more and more distant like an old memory. They would not forget, but instead use the knowledge of its whereabouts.

"How far?" Jemma questioned Eddie who was still staring off into the distance.

"I'd say no more than half a click due northeast," he replied.

"Then let's get a move on!" Jemma ordered.

She was about to start marching towards the area when Eddie placed a hand on her small shoulder. He could feel she was tense and quickly let go. "Shouldn't we think about our plan of action?"

Jemma smiled. "Now's your chance to prove yourself, Mr. Journalist."

Eddie stared dumbfounded.

"We need to hurry," Agwa said. "We may lose track of the smoke once it's done dissipating."

Jemma carried on and Agwa followed, sticking close to her sister. Eddie took up the rear and was quickly outpaced by them. He looked around for anything that could support his weight and found a big enough stick to use to carry himself with.

The jungle was as thick as ever as the three pressed on. The sweltering heat was even making Agwa sweat a bit. Jemma seemed to have adapted to the climate, as if she was immune to perspiration. They were about a quarter of a mile into their hike when they found a clearing.

Burn marks covered the area where the long grass once stood. A huge, singed circumference surrounded the area. There was no doubt that they were at the scene of the explosion. There was still some greenery left. The turf was burnt, and it looked like someone had lit a freshly mowed lawn on fire. Further out were the remnants of the fireball. Some tall grass, some sticks and rocks.

What immediately caught Eddie's eyes first though was the body of Ace Whitaker. He was burnt to a crisp but was clearly not killed by the explosion. The top of his head had been taken off with some small fragments of brain scattered around his cranium. They were on fire, crackling as they were being cooked on a hot stove.

While he investigated the deceased POW, Jemma and Agwa noticed something else. A heap of sticks were rising and falling as if someone was trying to get out from under them. A charred hand reached over them and was seemingly trying to pull the sticks off.

Their eyes widened. It had to be either Vinnie or Daniel. They secretly hoped for the latter. The sisters ran over and began to pull the fallen foliage off the body. Finally seeing more than just a hand, Jemma froze. It wasn't either one of them but one of Se-hun's men. He did not look human anymore though. He had misshapen features, and his face was bulkier, more defined.

She stopped digging him out when she noticed the teeth. They were triangular like a shark's. Agwa didn't see them until it was too late. The zombified soldier reached out and took her wrist in a vice-like grip.

Her scream caught Eddie's attention and he bolted over just in time to see one of Se-hun's men bite into Agwa's arm. Her blood-curdling scream sent immediate shivers down his spine.

Meanwhile, Jemma was backing up and raising her AK47 at the monster man. She positioned her shot, aiming right for the head, and fired. He fell backwards, hitting his head on the ground with a resounding *thump*.

Eddie charged over and grabbed Agwa and pulled her away. He then sat her down and looked over her arm. "Are you alright?"

"It stings!" she sobbed.

Jemma walked over and looked down at her sister's arm which was already beginning to pulsate with infection.

"I don't want to be like them!"

"We don't know if that will happen," Eddie stated.

"I've seen the infection spread when the tree shark did it to others. This will be no different!" Agwa cried.

Jemma too began to shed tears.

"I can wrap it up and we'll get the hell out of here," Eddie told her.

"Or we can just cut her arm off." Anton approached from behind Eddie.

"What the fuck!" Eddie turned around only to be punched in the face.

He hit the ground and Anton quickly made his way over to Agwa. Jemma was about to intervene when she felt a weapon press against her back. She heard Se-hun chuckle behind her.

"I thought I killed you!" she said, baffled.

"You should have aimed lower, for my heart." "You don't have one!"

"You've got me there."

Agwa quickly raised the colt commander and pointed it directly at Anton who was fast enough to snatch it out of her weakened grip.

"I'll be taking that," Anton chuckled.

Climbing over her, Anton then held Agwa down by her forearm. "This'll hurt you more than it'll hurt me."

"No!" Jemma cried out, dropping her AK47 in shock.

He raised his scimitar and brought it down with incredible force. It severed the arm at the elbow immediately. Agwa writhed in pain as Anton got off her and quickly found a smoldering stick. He pressed it against the stub and cauterized the wound. Her shrieks caused Jemma to become enraged, and she was about to spin around and do something, anything, to finally kill Se-hun. She was able to compose herself enough to stay in place.

Eddie finally came around just in time to have Agwa's arm tossed at him. He looked up at Anton, seething, his eyes like piercing daggers looking directly into the Russian's.

Anton paid him no mind and made his way over to Se-hun. He then handed him the small weapon. "I believe this is yours, Commander."

Se-hun smiled and took it. He then backed away and told Jemma to turn around. She was baffled to see that he didn't have a weapon on her at all. He was just using his fingers in the shape of an imaginary barrel.

Anton then took the revolver from Eddie and ignored the discarded AK47 on the ground.

"Alright, gang. Let's go check out that base," Se-hun chuckled.

***

At first glance, the structure was seemingly abandoned. A haze of heat swept across the jungle landscape. As Se-hun led the others, their feet kicked up vapors of marsh gas. Oddly enough, the building was placed close enough to a swamp to be subject to some of its conditions. It was not muddy though. Thick puffs of seemingly uprooted grass flattened as they pressed down on them.

Anton hated to say it but as he brought up the rear it all appeared to be unnatural. The terrain didn't belong in the jungle or anywhere else in the world for that matter. It was as if an alien made this area its otherworldly home.

Jemma cradled Agwa as the two walked side by side. Eddie was in front of them. Not by choice. He'd rather be by their side to protect them from all visible angles. He did not have a choice in the matter.

"How could you?" Jemma finally spoke through barely parted lips.

Eddie was about to turn when he caught Se-hun's head twitch slightly back so he stayed looking forward.

"I asked you a question."

"It wasn't my fault. I would've protected you both had I not been caught off guard."

"I'm sure," Jemma said sarcastically.

"Enough chitchat," Se-hun hissed.

As some of the fog began to lift, they noticed more and more of the area. The infrastructure of the concrete building was smashed in on one side on the second floor. Below was an entanglement of vines. They seemed to have been attached to something at one point.

Soon they came upon a couple of doors.

Se-hun wasted no time in pushing them open. As he did so, he kicked up a gust of mist that now hovered high over his head. He examined the inside. It was dark, near pitch black save for a small orange glow at the other end of the hall.

He walked through the entrance, as did the others.

"Call out to your friends."

"Rex? Daniel?" Eddie said softly. He figured they would have to be here. Ace was dead but the others could still be alive. "Saber? Vinnie?"

"Louder, idiot!" Anton shoved him from behind.

"Guys, it's us. Eddie, Jemma, and Agwa. We're okay, we're alive."

He didn't want to make it seem they deliberately split up. Even though they didn't, Se-Hun could make it even worse than before if he knew that help was on the way.

"C'mon, guys! We're here. Please answer."

"Why weren't you with them to begin with?" Anton chimed in.

Shit.

"We were patrolling the area and got separated from the group when the creature attacked. I assume they ended up here," Eddie explained while doing a poor job of hiding the fact that he was lying.

"Really." Se-hun chuckled as he turned around slowly. "Why would you and two young women be patrolling the area? I mean, surely, we didn't treat Daniel-San and his men bad enough to warrant them having civilians caught in the middle of such a predicament."

"I beg to differ." Jemma then added, "They're lucky they can still stand after shooting guns after what you and your *men* put then through."

"*Anjing*!" he hushed her in her native, Chinese language.

Just then there was a groaning sound. It was coming from behind one of the nearby doors. Enough light cast upon it to reveal a handle as well as a small porthole. Se-hun quickly marched over and looked through the tiny window. Through it he saw a familiar face across the room.

"Daniel-San!"

Anton perked up after hearing this. His whole demeanor changed from serious to enticed.

Se-hun saw his Russian accomplice in the reflection and smiled. He turned around and looked at him with a smirk. “Officer Morosov, it’s time.”

He quickly made his way around Jemma, Agwa, and Eddie and to the Korean commander. “It’ll be my pleasure.”

“No!” Jemma cried out.

Agwa was barely lucid but got the implications of what was about to go down. “Please don’t. Not after all me and my sister have been through.”

“That’s what’ll make his death so much sweeter,” Anton sneered as he opened the door by spinning the dog handle and quickly stepping inside, sealing himself in.

“You’re going to burn in hell for this!” Eddie shouted.

“Can’t be much worse than this place.” Se-hun smiled and then took Eddie by the arm and rushed him and the Reyes sisters past him. “Now, let’s go find your friends.”

CHAPTER ELEVEN

The grim dark.

With rays of light coming from above in small slivers, the room was mostly shrouded in shadows. The rafters shook as the air vents turned on. Anton smiled as he stared down at the pitiful man before him. He had obviously had enough. To Anton that couldn't be further from the truth. He was going to make him suffer.

Daniel had singe marks on his face and most of the hair on his exposed chest and genitals were burnt off. He stared at the Russian before him with disdain. There wasn't much of a fight he could put up against the man who was built and toned into a perfect figure.

As a cool rush of air filtered through the system, Daniel took a deep breath. Anton was already sizing him up and it wouldn't be long before their combat would begin. He just hoped that the ruthless killer would deal a fatal blow quickly.

"You should really be quieter." Anton gave an almost friendly smile. "You gave away your position so carelessly.""How do you know it wasn't intentional?" Daniel chuckled.

"Ha!" Anton scoffed. "You think I buy that you have a plan. I could've taken all five of you down back at base camp last night."

"But you didn't," Daniel said.

Anton stood silent.

"You wanted me all for yourself," Daniel continued. "You can't stand me, can you? You can't handle that I've kept my composure all this time. You just want to see my pain. Well, newsflash, I'm an internal crier."

"We'll see about that." Anton raised his scimitar and charged for Daniel.

There was no warning. Anton went in for the attack, his weapon raised high above his head.

Daniel was quick though and brought his foot up, giving him a swift upward kick to the groin.

Knees buckled, Anton fell down. Through gritted teeth he looked up at his prisoner.

"I also cheat like a dirty bastard when the time comes for me to." Daniel grinned and got to his feet.

He then brought one foot down to step on Anton's bald head.

Anton quickly shimmied out of the way. Sharp pain spread up Daniel's leg like a bolt of lightning striking a tree. He backed off and nearly fell down on his rear. Suddenly, another wave of agonizing grief came to him in the form of the scimitar sticking into his shoulder.

He hollered and tried to back up but there was nowhere to go. There was a thirty foot drop off the catwalk.

As Anton plunged the blade deeper, a single tear fell from Daniel's eye.

"Oh, I thought you didn't want to be seen crying?"

"I was more referring to hiding the pain of my brother's death," Daniel said through gritted teeth.

"You're an emotional bastard, aye? Well, I guess you'll be seeing your brother soon."

The blade slid out of Daniel's shoulder like butter. A wet, suction sound could be heard as it left his body. Anton then raised the scimitar over his head. Daniel closed his eyes and muttered a prayer.

Anton laughed heartedly and then lunged forward, the blade coming down to slice Daniel's head in half. He stopped suddenly when he felt something removed from his side. There was the cocking sound of Eddie's revolver as Anton turned around and saw Vinnie standing there.

"Burn in hell," Daniel finished praying.

An explosion of skull fragments and blood flew away from the side of Anton's cranium, and he collapsed. A copious amount of viscera and brain matter spilled from the hole in his head, a seemingly never-ending gushing geyser.

Looking up, Daniel saw Vinnie standing there.

He gave a hoop and holler. "You see?! That's what happens when you give me a gun!"

Unbelievably, Anton began to get up. His head was hung low and one of his eyes seemed to want to pop out of his head. He was not down for the count though.

Without hesitation, Vinnie put his hands up in a boxer's stance, keeping them held in front of his face to block and defend himself from incoming blows. "I am Vinnie Moretti, boxing champ of Italy's very own underground rings! I will not yield."

Anton just smirked, bloody spittle drooling from his lower lip as he growled, "Let's dance, Mister Champ."

Bringing his arm around wide, Anton swung high over Vinnie's head. His smaller opponent then went in for a quick jab, but he was already bringing his other hand in from the right. It caught Vinnie off guard. He did not expect fast decision making and sharp reflexes from a man with half the top of his head gone.

The punch sent Vinnie nearly falling off the catwalk. He tried to push himself, forcing his body forward but he kept leaning further and further back.

Anton saw this as his golden opportunity. It would be a quick fight after all.

Vinnie managed to regain his footing and used his whole body to propel forward. His fist clenched, he brought it square into Anton's face. Some blood squirted from the wound, further staining his bald head red.

He stumbled back, cradling his head with his hand. It was in that moment, Anton knew that this fight was pointless. He had to get his hands on the revolver. As his vision cleared a bit, he saw Vinnie standing near the ledge. He was dangling the weapon with his index finger over the side.

"I won't be needing this."

With a half-hearted toss, the revolver flung from his finger and began its descent into the pitch-black pit.

"*Gahhhh!*" Anton screamed and then charged for Vinnie.

An arm slipped around his chest and, before Anton even realized what was going on, the blade of his scimitar was dragged across his throat. He quickly reached for the gaping wound. Each pulsating spasm sent more crimson substance pouring from the slash. There was no more air that would be accessible to his lungs. The only thing that came out was gurgling.

Swiftly kicking the back of Anton's leg, Daniel grabbed Anton by the shoulders and turned the downed man. The Russian looked at his former prisoner who held the blade up, victorious.

"And you won't be needing this." Daniel smiled.

He then shoved him off the catwalk and he disappeared into the grim, dark void.

Daniel wanted to cheer, get up and hug his comrade and all his newfound courage. It was all cut short when a lanky arm-like appendage burst through Vinnie's stomach. Crimson matter erupted from the exit wound. He drooled red saliva and looked down at the fatal wound.

The wooden claws slowly raked back, carving out entrails and innards that came spilling out of his back.

"No!" Daniel cried out.

Vinnie barely muttered audibly but it was clear what he was trying to say. *Run.*

Quickly getting to his feet, Daniel almost fell back again. He managed to catch himself on the railing and then slowly inched away from the tree shark that had impaled his fellow soldier, his brother in arms.

The creature snarled at him over Vinnie's shoulder.

He nearly froze with fear but managed to snap out of it enough to inch further to the door behind him. Slowly reaching down, he managed to get a grip on the dog handle and get a few turns when the creature ripped the rest of its arm out of Vinnie's back and swiftly tossed his lifeless corpse over the railing.

It then charged for him.

Daniel took both hands and spun the wheel until he heard a click and pushed through the doorway. He nearly fell as the creature took a swipe at him. The claws practically touched the thin hair on the top of his head. Before he could hit the ground, he put both hands out and pushed himself upward. He then ran.

As it tried to get through the small doorway, the tree shark was quickly deciding to abandon the prey. The frame of the passageway would require strenuous work to break. He was already two rooms ahead of it.

It had lost interest and decided to go back the way it came. Sticking its claws on his hands and feet into the wall for support, the monstrosity ascended until it reached the rafters and found one of the windows above them that it came through. It gripped the glass frame, paying no attention to the pain generated from the shards stabbing into its palms.

Soon, it was on a stable part of the roof. It scoured the area. There were many other entry points from windows and even some open shafts. It carefully placed its steps to avoid stepping on any thin windowpanes and proceeded to search for its next kill.

***

Agwa screamed uncontrollably. The bodies of Rex and a woman were enough to send shivers down her back. She nearly fainted. Se-hun paid the corpses no mind nor her shrieks of fear and disgust. Instead, he was busy assessing the situation.

It looked like one of them was working on the radio, perhaps trying to fix it. Broken debris littered the floor. There were apparent signs that something climbed up to the second floor to gain access and kill them. Se-hun silently hoped they didn't reach anyone before the creature got them.

A thought, or rather a memory, crossed his mind then. The reporter was acting very suspicious when asked about the reason for their whereabouts.

"Turn around." Se-hun faced Eddie.

"What? Why?" he replied.

"Do not make me repeat myself or I'll blow your brains out." Se-hun unholstered his colt commander.

Eddie wasted no time and turned around. He then patted him down. He managed to locate a few rolls of film and some gum. It wasn't until he checked his vest that he noticed the knob. He pulled out the damaged radio.

"What the fuck is this?!"

"I, uh. . ."

"Did you make contact with an escort out of here?!" Se-hun was screaming.

Eddie's eyes were shifting, looking everywhere but at the commander. "No, we tried but couldn't get through. The thing's toast!"
"Bullshit!" Se-hun shouted inches from Eddie's face.

He then turned to Agwa. "If you, Mister Reporter, don't tell me the truth, I'll blow her shoulder out and she'll lose use of both arms."

"No!" Jemma cried out.

She tried to jump in the way, but Eddie moved in front of her. "Ok, I'll tell you everything."

Se-hun smiled but still kept the gun trained on Agwa. "See? That wasn't so hard, was it?"

Jemma looked up as if to pray to God. She noticed something looking at them from the windowpane. It was one of those tree sharks.

"We need to go," she said softly.

"We're not going anywhere until Mister Reporter here calls in to cancel the pick-up." Se-hun grinned from ear to ear.

"I already told you, the radio's no good!"

"Then she'll need someone to feed her for the rest of her life!" Se-hun snarled.

"You really are a bastard," Eddie said coldly.

There was a cracking sound. It was high pitched as if something was about to shatter. Se-hun looked up to the origin of the noise and saw the creature staring at them.

Eddie took this opportunity to charge him. He managed to get ahold of his wrist with the gun in it. The weapon fired, missing Agwa's head by a few inches. As they struggled, the creature pounded down on the glass.

Jemma quickly grabbed her sister and, together, they hid under a nearby desk.

Fragments of glass fell from the ceiling as the two men fought. With the window broken, the creature hopped down just as Eddie shoved Se-hun away. The commander of the prison camp pointed the colt commander at him. "What does it matter, you'll all be dead before your rescue gets here anyway."

Slam.

The tree shark plummeted right onto Se-hun and immediately began to punch its claws into his stomach.

Maneuvering around the feasting, Eddie held a hand out to Jemma and Agwa. The two were soon by his side and running out of the radio room.

As they ran down each stair, two at a time, the hallway came into view. They kept going; the entrance wasn't too far. Eddie stopped dead in his tracks. There was one of the zombies blocking their escape.

"No!" Eddie said bitterly.

A shot rang out. It came from right next to them. Agwa stood there with Se-hun's colt commander in hand. She had seemingly grabbed the presumably discarded weapon as they ran out of the room.

Blood squirted from the zombie's neck. He noticed them now and began to make his way towards them.

She went to take another shot, but nothing came out. The gun jammed.

Suddenly, a figure of a man came out from behind the zombie. He wrapped his arm around the undead corpse's neck and placed his other hand atop his head. Then, he quickly pulled back, snapping the zombie's neck. His head fell off and Saber stood there with it hanging from his hand.

"Hell yeah!" Eddie cheered.

A hand was placed on his shoulder.

He spun around and saw that Daniel was behind him. "We need to get out of here!"
"You don't have to tell us twice!" Eddie said.

"I vote we level this place with the creature inside," Daniel suggested. "I went to the radio room and locked it. If we can blow it up, we may be done with this whole mess and be home free."

"We don't have explosives," Eddie said.

"No, but we can set the place on fire. There's bound to be something flammable in here. It's our best bet."

"I'll help," Agwa said.

"No, you, Jemma, and Eddie wait outside. Me and Saber can handle this."

As Daniel and Saber worked on finding a flammable source inside the structure, the others were making their way across the compound. Agwa was between Eddie and Jemma who were trying to carry her. She was feeling woozy and almost collapsed a few times as they crossed the yard. A few more yards and they sat her down near the fence where she fell into a deep sleep. Jemma looked to Eddie who was checking over her sister's wound. He was being delicate and patient with the injury. It was obviously getting infected, so he ripped off a piece of his shirt and wrapped it up. He covered the nub to keep dirt out of it.

Jemma began to reflect and feel guilty of what she had thought and said to the man. He had been honest and kept his word to protect them. She felt a sudden urge of respect for him. She wanted to return the favor but, deep down, felt that he'd reject that notion.

"I'm sorry," she said.

"Don't be."

"You have every right to be mad at me."

"I'm not." He turned to her. "I'm just glad that you're both okay."

She blushed and then noted his handiwork. "You're good at patching her up."

"I've patched up guys bleeding on war grounds throughout my career. This is nothing compared to trying to glue somebody's open stomach while pushing the guts back in."

Eddie noticed she shivered at the thought. "Sorry."

There was silence.

"Once we get out of here, I'm going to get you and your sister away from this horrible place."

She smiled. "Where would we go?"

Eddie thought about it for a moment. "I have an apartment. It's a bit cramped but it's a home." He looked sheepishly at her. "Maybe you and your sister would. . ."

Without hesitation, she leaned over and kissed him on the cheek. The song, *Piece of My Heart* by Janice Joplin came to mind and played out in his head. His whole demeanor changed and there was a glow that seemed to radiate from him.

"I'd love that." She gave another sweet smile.

The butterflies disappeared from within, and he gained a new confidence. It was like his whole world was full of bright red roses and the sweet smell of honey suckle.

"Finally," Agwa groaned through half-open eyes and with a grin.

The two laughed as Saber and Daniel approached.

"There's a boat waiting for us," Daniel explained.

"What about setting the place on fire?" Eddie asked.

Just then, glass shattered, and flames burst out of one of the windows. Smoke began to rise and fill the area.

“I see,” Eddie said.

“Come on, let’s go,” Daniel said.

Saber took over Jemma’s spot and he and Eddie helped carry Agwa.

CHAPTER TWELVE

Familiarity.

The sounds of the jungle were coming back. Silence had befallen the green hell when the gas tank erupted. Now, as the building's infrastructure began to break apart and collapse into itself, the area seemed to explode with a bombastic reverberation of racket. While the flames rose higher, so too did the frequency of animal noises.

Certain insects were stridulating while birds cooed and cawed. Some of the larger frogs gave deep, throaty croaks while others gave almost a small chirping sound. There were even some faint hissing noises as if even the snakes rejoiced in the destruction of the makeshift laboratory.

As the remaining group made their way towards the beach, the sun seemed to cast into the jungle, punctuating the greens and yellowish browns. It was as if the whole sky was glowing. They had done a service, not only to the nation, but to the world.

Eddie couldn't help but look behind him as he and Saber carried Agwa. At first, he was smiling at Jemma who returned the gesture. Then, he looked past her. The building seemed miles away. He knew they were only a football field in length from the grounds though.

Daniel had taken point. He was beginning to register a faint whirring sound when the memory of the familiar series of quick chops returned to him. It was when he and Se-hun's men were returning to the base. Se-hun had had the last laugh when the helicopter passed over them.

"How close did your chopper come to the camp, Stokes?" Daniel asked the reporter.

"Too close. I told them to hold back but it was too late."

"I hope you didn't see the brigade heading back to it?"

Eddie was silent only momentarily. "I did see you. We all saw you. Believe me when I say that if we had intervened then you would've most likely been shot in the crossfire."

"I understand." Daniel figured now was not the time to argue on strategy.

By the time they had reached the mile-mark, the group were out of ear shot. There was a shifting in the piling rubble. A wooden arm reached out from the pieces of wood and chunks of concrete. It tried to reach for anything to aid in it being able to pull itself out. It found flesh instead.

Se-hun stood there. The creature's claws were digging into his foot. Entrails were hanging out of his stomach and yet he smiled. Soon he found himself laughing. His veins were replaced with vines as his genetic makeup was intruded with seeds.

He saw the downed creature before him and reached forward. There was no pain in his abdomen. Instead, the stretching motion felt satisfactory. It was as if he was enjoying his innards falling out and his skin ripping apart.

Grabbing the head of the tree shark, he pulled back and twisted it. He struggled only slightly as the top half of the creature came apart. Se-hun fell backwards and bellowed with entertained laughter. He looked up and saw the whites of the creature's eyes. Peering past the body's mass, he saw his midsection and legs still standing where he once stood. He hollered with a roaring cheer.

They were soon replaced with vines that shot out of his upper torso. It felt like noodles slipping down his throat and into his stomach. He soon found them to be useful in picking him up. When he was upright, he nearly fell forward but managed to compose his stance. He then looked down at the vines, like a thousand tentacles whipping around.

A new sensation then came over him. He could smell the others nearby. Namely Agwa's singed flesh.

Before the others could step foot on the sand, Saber fell to his knees. Agwa nearly landed on the ground herself but Eddie held her up.

Daniel and Jemma rushed to the Filipino's aid. He was convulsing uncontrollably. Foamy saliva began to spill from his dry lips. His eyes rolled back, exposing their whites. He pounded his fist on the dirt, inches from the converging sand.

"Not this again!" Daniel shouted.

"What's he doing?" Agwa cried out.

"This happened when the monster was near."

"Are they connected somehow?" Jemma inquired.

"I don't think so." Daniel then explained as he gripped Saber's hand. "When he came in from the Vietnam campaign, Saber and I disposed of a supposed enemy village. There, he stumbled upon a shaman who was later executed. I didn't see the whole ritual. I only caught the tail end of it. Needless to say, seeing him like this made me believe in supernatural occurrences."

"If he's sensing that thing, then there's got to be another one," Eddie stated.

"Who knows how many more there actually are?!" Daniel shouted.

"Can we please get out of here?" Agwa asked.

"Go!" Saber screamed at Daniel, startling everyone. "He's coming."

"I'm not leaving you, man!" Daniel cried out.

Saber looked to Jemma, then to Agwa, then back to Daniel. "They risked their lives for you. It's time for you to do the same."

Daniel shed a tear and then grabbed Saber's shoulder, giving it a reassuring squeeze. "I will never forget you."

"Nor I you," Saber said coldly.

The sounds of trees cracking and collapsing could be heard in the distance.

Daniel looked at Saber. "To hell and back."

Saber smiled. "To the bitter end, I fight. You live."

Jemma quickly got up and rushed to Daniel's side. She then helped him to his feet and they joined Eddie and Agwa who were already down on the beach.

***

The radio was alive with the *woo* and *hoos* of Chester Arthur Burnett as he sang *Smokestack Lightning*. Roger and Lennie had been calmed with the aid of music and the soft lapsing of wavelets on the boat's hull.

"I always liked Howlin' Wolf," Lennie said.

"Mmm," Roger agreed. "He's definitely got a unique style."

They had been watching the beach for a couple of hours now. The sand seemed to shift unnaturally from time to time. A trick of the eye. Roger half expected Lennie to scream that a naked woman was on the beach via a mirage.

"When do you think they'll get here?" Lennie asked.

"I don't know, man. Just enjoy some tunes. They're helping take the edge off both of us."

"Wow, for the first time since we came to this awful place, you want me to *enjoy* myself?!"

"It's not like you've indulged in anything else since we got here. Besides maybe scoffing down all our food."

"Fuck you, Roge'!"

The two sat in silence momentarily.

"I think we should just get out of here," Roger suggested.

"What about Barbra and the others?" Lennie was visibly shaking, shocked at his colleague's proposal.

Roger turned to him. "Someone has to make it and, I for one . . ."

"Hey! Look at that girl!" Lennie pointed down at the beach.

Oh boy, I called it, Roger thought to himself.

It wasn't until he looked at the beach for himself that he too noticed the girl. She was accompanied by a man of Lennie's size, maybe a bit smaller. Close behind them was another female, a woman, and Daniel Stout.

"Holy shit! They made it!" Lennie cheered. "Holy shit!"

A tremendous force came crashing through the palm trees behind them. The top half was of a Korean soldier who was seemingly undergoing some kind of bodily change. The bottom half was a tentacle-fused nightmare.

"What the actual fuck!" Roger muttered under his breath.

The abomination quickly changed direction and charged into the surf. The water splashed and waves broke against its thick body. Worst of all, it was coming for them.

"Get the boat started!" Lennie screamed like a little girl.

Roger reached into his pocket and fumbled for the keys. Finally getting a firm grip on them, he ripped his hand from his pocket. On the way out, the keys got snagged on a thin strand of cotton. When Roger yanked again, the keys went flying upward.

Quick as a rabbit, Roger's reflexes and instinctive nature took over and he shot his hand out to grab them. He felt them hit his hand and then slip through his fingers. He held out his other cupped hand below. The keys were mere inches away when they passed it and landed in the ocean.

"Oh shit," Roger whimpered.

Woo hoo.

"I knew it!" Daniel shouted. "I knew it could swim!"

"No shit, it's part shark," Eddie added.

Daniel ignored the jab and watched as Roger fumbled with the keys. They then fell into the ocean and a look of utter defeat crossed the man's dark face.

"Where the hell is that chopper?!" Daniel demanded.

"It should be here!" Eddie exclaimed. "It's probably just circling around. Maybe they didn't see us on the last pass."

"I hope you're right," Daniel said. "Because if they don't get here in the next few minutes, our fate will end up just like theirs." He pointed over his shoulder.

The song had begun to fade out when it fell off the dashboard and onto the deck below, smashing into pieces. Lennie paid no mind as he scrambled to hide in the deck below. Roger dug into one of the nearby compartments and produced the grenade. He quickly pulled the pin and tossed it towards the incoming foe.

Water erupted right next to the creature as shrapnel fragments sliced into it. What little humanity was left of Se-hun's face was one of excitement. He was laughing at their efforts, smiling at their defeat.

Rows of wooden teeth looked like the tips of a carved spear. The concept of the species would've been humorous if it weren't so terrifying to look at. Roger closed his eyes as the creature smashed into the hull and reached up with its vines. Before he could grab one of the M16s, they wrapped around his neck and squeezed, forcing Roger to open his eyes.

He stared at it. The Korean's face was still there but the mouth was elongated. Suddenly, the pressure around Roger's neck loosened. He thought it was giving him relief. It was short-lived as it made him watch as the last bits of human appearance ripped away to reveal the horrible monstrosity beneath.

Tightening its grip, the vines were like razors, slicing deeper and deeper until Roger's head rolled off his body and a copious amount of blood erupted from the stump.

It then took hold of his lifeless corpse and flung it over the side.

Below, Lennie cowered in the corner. The only light came from the port holes. Above him was a bullseye window. He tried to calculate if he could fit. It was his only chance of escape.

As he got up, he saw tentacles covering the floor. At first, he thought an octopus had come to attack the boat as well. It dawned on him that they were just the vines of the tree shark and he screamed.

"No!"

He reached up and pushed the hatch open. Squeezing his stomach in as much as humanly possible, he managed to get his arms and head through. He was making slow progress, but he realized he might be able to actually fit all the way through.

A pair of wooden jaws came down and bit on his upper half. His gargled cries were cut short when the creature pulled him upward and chomped down. His lower half hit the cabin floor and the vines began to cut and tear at his skin and innards.

They gave up when they realized the remaining carcass wouldn't have a chance at life without a heart or brain.

Eddie sat Agwa down. Jemma came over and held her close. The three huddled together, awaiting whatever outcome would occur. This was their last resort.

Daniel was not finished. He needed to see this thing through. To dispose of the creature and finally go home. His war may never be over, but this'd be a fulfilling start.

The four watched as the creature smashed the boat into the water, further capsizing it. Unsatisfied until it was no longer seaworthy, it spun it hull-side-up and began to bash into it again.

After it was pleased with its destructive butchery, the tree shark slid off the hull and began to swim back towards shore. It was on the beach in twelve seconds. At fifteen seconds it towered over the group.

No one, not even the creature itself, registered the sound of the whirring helicopter nearby.

"What in the Sam hell?!" the pilot shouted.

The second pilot quickly unfastened his seatbelt and ran to the rail gun mounted on the left side of the chopper. With quick maneuvering, they were angled directly at their target.

A barrage of bullets exploded from the weapon and into the monstrosity before them. Yellow blood erupted from its skin as small tungsten missiles pelted its thick hide, puncturing through it with ease.

On the ground, the four watched in awe. It was as if it were screaming in agony and pain in slow motion. The creature's head swayed back and forth as it was riddled with lead from the ammunition.

Yet there was no sound coming from it. It was dying without being able to cry out.

Despite one of the most vicious Korean prison camp commanders being the host for this organism, it came to Eddie's attention that it was just trying to survive. It was created in a lab. It was never meant to be.

Soon, it was visibly weakened to the point where it couldn't support its own weight anymore and it slumped over. Bark stained with yellow blood was scattered all around the back of it. It had been chipped away on the back, leaving its prey relatively clean and unscathed.

For now.

CHAPTER THIRTEEN

Lost and Found.

Once the threat was disposed of, the pilots began to circle the beach. Eddie and Jemma helped Agwa up as Daniel began to approach the landing chopper. A great sense of weight came off him. His relief was only the beginning. He knew that he would have to live with so much for the rest of his life.

He had lost his entire squad, not only to the creature, not only to the Vietcong, but to the war itself. It had all been so pointless even though it was over. There was a wife for him back home to help him pick up the pieces. The burden he'd place on her would not be true to his character. He would need time to heal. No mortal human could replace time.

The landing rails touched the sand about the same time the co-pilot raised a rifle. Daniel stopped dead in his tracks while Eddie got in front of Jemma and Agwa.

"Freeze!" the man said louder than he needed to.

No one moved.

"I said freeze!" he repeated.

Still, everyone remained still.

A shot was fired.

It hit its target.

Saber fell to the ground. Daniel spun around.

"No!"

Eddie looked to where Saber was now lying in a pool of blood. He then turned to the co-pilot. "Oh you fucking idiot."

Daniel rushed to his friend's side. His last comrade in this hellish place. The Filipino was gripping the side of his neck, his eyes practically bulging from their sockets.

"He's going into shock!" Daniel cried out.

The other pilot saw what happened and reached for a first aid kit.

Saber stared into Daniel's eyes. He then muttered something. It was in a different language that he couldn't understand. "Toca po," he repeated, clearly this time.

He then grabbed Daniel's shoulder and gave it a reassuring squeeze. "Goodbye, my friend."

By the time the pilot came over with the supplies, Saber was already dead.

It was as if time stopped. No one said a word, made a movement. Not even the once lively jungle made a peep.

Then, without warning, Daniel stood up. He arched his aching back and screamed a primal cry of rage and defiance towards the sky.

When he regained his senses, he looked down at Saber. After a few minutes, he turned around. He paid no mind to either pilot but, instead, marched past them and towards the helicopter.

Eddie turned to the murderer. "You're going to be court marshaled for this."

"I didn't know! For Christ's sake, they all look alike to me!"

"I see racism is alive and well in America," Jemma said.

"Of course," Eddie said. "And idiots who don't know about gun safety."

The three made their way towards the chopper and got in. The two pilots followed close behind.

On the aircraft, a familiar song to Daniel began to play. John Denver's sweet voice came on as *Sunshine on my Shoulders* came to life.

Eddie sat between the sisters; each had a head on either one of his shoulders. He kissed the top of Jemma's head and she snuggled against him. Agwa was already asleep.

"What do we do now?" Eddie asked.

Daniel looked out at the setting sun. "We go home."

"That was our home." Jemma glanced down below.

"That was just a place. A home is where the heart is," Eddie explained.

Daniel placed a hand on his heart. "Let's not forget those who won't be going home with us. My squad is gone. My brother is gone. May they always be remembered, never forgotten."

"They won't be," Eddie said as he looked down at his equipment that was on the floor.

"You didn't take any pictures of us."

"I didn't take any pictures of them, no. I didn't get a chance to take pictures of the past. But I can for the future." He smiled.

Daniel reached forward and took out the Nikon. He pointed it at the trio. “Let the future begin today.”

A flash lit up the cabin and a memory was created.

***

They stood watching the helicopter leave. As Chau examined the creature, Lam was pacing back and forth. His ear began to bleed again. The other two men were still sitting in the truck.

“Is this what it’s come to?!” Lam exploded.

“You wanted to come ‘in style’.” Chau made air quotes. “You should have brought a rocket launcher and not your whole damn torture chamber.”

Lam charged over to the back of the truck and pulled out what appeared to be a potato peeler but wider and sharper. “I’m going to make them bleed.”

“Good luck,” Chau chuckled.

One of the men in the truck put down his binoculars then pointed towards the sky. “The side of the chopper says brown eagle. The coding suggests it was originally stationed in Vietnam. Can’t be too far away.”

“They’ll need to land soon.” Lam smiled. He then turned to Chau. “Just what is the big bastard?”

“I’d say it’s part tree, part shark, and part Se-hun.”

“What?” Lam inquired impatiently.

“He either morphed into this thing or they combined with his cells. Either way, it’s a genetic marvel.”

Lam nodded and then looked over the creature. “We need a new army.”

“It’s too unethical,” Chau argued.

“So was the whole goddamned war and yet it still happened.” Lam then smiled. “Let’s restart, shall we?”

THE END

Check out other great

Cryptid Novels!

Ian Faulkner

CRYPTID

Be careful what you look for. You might just find it.1996. A group of 14 students walked into the trackless virgin forests of Graham Island, British Columbia for a three-day hike. They were never seen again. 2019. An American TV crew retrace those students' steps to attempt to solve a 23-year-old mystery.A disparate collection of characters arrives on the island. But all is not as it seems. Two of them carry dark secrets. Terrible knowledge that will mean death for some – but a fighting chance of survival for others. In the hidden depths of the forests – man is on the menu. Some mysteries should remain unsolved...

Eric S. Brown

LOCH NESS HORROR

The Order of the Eternal Light, a secret organization have foretold the end of the human race. In order to save all humanity, agents of the Order must locate the Loch Ness Monster and obtain a sample of its blood for within in it is the key to stopping the apocalypse but finding the monster will be no easy task.

www.ingramcontent.com/pod-product-compliance
Lightning Source LLC
Chambersburg PA
CBHW061243170626
46809CB00007B/2807

9781923165069